The Puffin
DO IT YOURSELF BOOK

Written and produced by
McPhee Gribble Publishers

With illustrations by David Lancashire and Jenny Elliott

D1132750

A Puffin Book

Puffin Books, Penguin Books Australia Ltd,
487 Maroondah Highway, P.O. Box 257
Ringwood, Victoria, 3134, Australia
Penguin Books Ltd,
Harmondsworth, Middlesex, England
Penguin Books,
40 West 23rd Street, New York, N.Y. 10010, U.S.A.
Penguin Books Canada Ltd,
2801 John Street, Markham, Ontario, Canada
Penguin Books (N.Z.) Ltd,
182–190 Wairau Road, Auckland 10, New Zealand

This collection first published by Penguin Books Australia, 1984
Written and produced by McPhee Gribble Publishers, Melbourne
Illustrated by David Lancashire and Jenny Elliott
Copyright © McPhee Gribble Publishers, 1984

Typeset in Plantin by Dudley E. King, Melbourne

Made and printed in Singapore by Tien Wah Press

CIP

The Puffin Do It Yourself Book

For children.
ISBN 0 14 031. 723 6

1. Play – Juvenile literature. 2. Games –
Juvenile literature. 3. Amusements – Juvenile
literature. I. Lancashire, David. II. Elliot, Jenny.
III. McPhee Gribble Publishers.

790.1'922

CONTENTS

Making Things 45

Exploring 85

Note for Parents and Teachers

The Puffin Do It Yourself Book introduces a new generation of children to projects from the highly successful Practical Puffin series – and a lot of new material too.

It is a book that encourages children to get out and investigate the world, to draw on their own resources, develop skills and make decisions about what they can tackle.

The warning or instructing adult voice is absent so that children will feel free to add their own ideas and be pleased with the results – however imperfect.

BODY TRICKS

HYPNOTIZED ARMS

Stand in a open doorway. Press the backs of both wrists as hard as you can against the door frame.

Press as if you are trying to raise your arms above your head – but the doorway is stopping you.

Count slowly to 50 pressing as hard as possible all the time.

Now walk away with your arms quite floppy and see what happens.

PARALYZED KNEE

Press all of one side of your body firmly against a wall.

Make sure the side of your foot is pressed against the wall too.

Now try to raise the other foot.

BODY BAND

A body band means just that. One person plays as many instruments as possible at the same time, and usually sings as well.

You can attach a drum to your back and play it with drumsticks tied to your elbows.

Cut a long strip of material about 8 cm wide and tie it firmly around the drum. Hold the drum in the small of your back. Bring the material around your waist and tie it in place.

Bells or a collection of spoons and tin lids can hang from the drum for extra noise.

A large biscuit tin makes a drum or use a toy.

You can attach saucepan lids to your knees for cymbals. Aluminium makes the best noise.

8

Long-handled wooden spoons can be held on to the inside of your elbows with elastic. If you move your elbows in and out you will hit the drum.

You may have to adjust the position of the sticks or the drum until the drumsticks hit the centre of the drum.

Bend a wire clothes hanger into this shape. You may need pliers and another pair of hands to help.

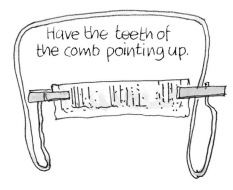

Have the teeth of the comb pointing up.

Put the wire tips through the end holes on each peg. Then hang the whole thing around your neck. Adjust it to fit. You need to be able to reach the comb by tilting your head forward slightly.

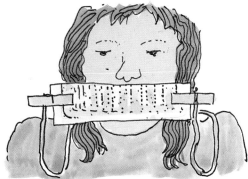

To play the hummerzoo your lips should only just touch the paper. Hum loudly.

Now you have three instruments to play. Your hands and feet are still free to use maraccas, a tambourine, or tap dance.

You will need lots of practice — but the sight and sound of you is worth the effort.

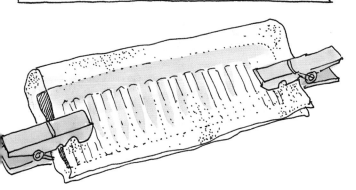

You can make a hummerzoo to wear on your shoulders. Fold a piece of tissue paper over a comb and trim the edges to fit. Hold it in place with a spring peg at each end.

BED TRICKS

Your bed can be full of surprises for other people. Make some extra limbs to have in bed with you.

Stuff a long pair of socks firmly. Put large shoes on them. Have them peeping out from the end of the bed.

An extra arm could appear from behind you. This could be a sweater sleeve stuffed with socks.

A rubber glove could be tied to it. Fill the glove with flour and fasten it tightly with a rubber band.

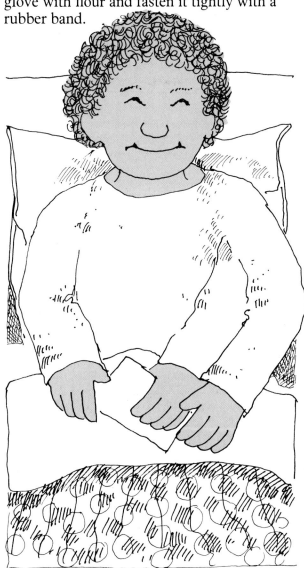

Make a bed serpent to slide and slither around you.

You need a strip of slippery material like satin.

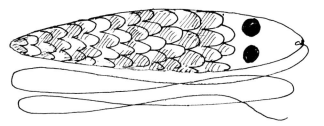

Cut it into a serpent shape. Draw on mean eyes and scales. Thread a long length of fine thread through the tip of the nose and tie a knot.

The serpent lies in wait at the end of the bed. Loop the free end of the thread around the back of your neck.

Wait till the right moment to pull the thread and bring your serpent slithering over the covers and up your arm.

It is easy to make a back view of you wrestling another body in your bed.

Lie face down with your head under the pillow. Wrap your arms tightly around you. Clutch at your shoulder blades and wrestle yourself.

11

MIDNIGHT FEASTS

Midnight feasts are usually held with other people — but you could have one by yourself.

A group feast needs a leader. Choose one wakeful person to be in charge of getting you all there. Staying awake can be harder than you think.

The place doesn't matter as long as it's secret. The time should be midnight. It's a magical time and feels right.

Food for a midnight feast needs to be special. Choose things you don't get to eat often during the day. Things that aren't too messy are best — or your secret will be known next day.

If you have a large thermos flask, you could store ice cream until you are ready to eat.

Hot frankfurts in a thermos work well too. They will cook if you pour very hot water over them and leave them for a few hours.

13

CLOCKWORK FACE

Practice doing this in front of a mirror. You need to be able to do it very fast and jerkily like a machine.

1 Twist an ear – which makes your tongue come out.

2 Pull your left ear – your tongue goes to the right.

3 Pull your right ear – your tongue goes to the left.

4 Wind your left ear very slowly – your tongue moves slowly to the right.

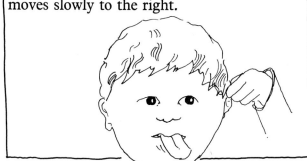

5 Wind your right ear very slowly – your tongue gets half way round and then gets jammed.

6 Press your nose with a finger – and your tongue snaps back in.

Slap the back of your neck – your tongue comes out and you can start again.

SEW YOURSELF UP

This is good for doing on buses or trains. You must imagine you are using a needle and thread – and don't laugh.

Watch closely when someone is sewing. See how they have to push the needle to get it through something tough.

They have to grip the point of the needle as it comes through the other side so they can pull it out. Then there is a little tug to pull the thread tight before the next stitch.

Thread an imaginary needle and make a big knot in imaginary thread.

You can pretend to sew each finger to the next until you can gather up your whole hand into a bunch.

Then try sewing through your lip or on to an ear. Maybe then you could sew your hand to the knee of your trousers.

Remember that it would hurt to be sewn up so pull faces too. People can almost see the needle when you get good at sewing yourself up.

CAMOUFLAGE

This means making yourself part of the scenery – so you can't be easily spotted.

In leafy places camouflaging yourself isn't hard. Twist stems into wreaths for your head and shoulders.

Carry a bunch of leaves to cover your face when necessary. Wear green and brown clothes and keep your body hidden in the bushes.

To camouflage yourself in open spaces, wear the disguise of something that might be found there.

Cut a peephole in a box large enough to sit inside. Wrap and label it to look like a parcel.

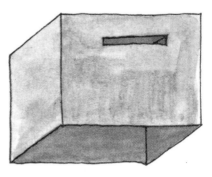

An old garbage bin makes another disguise. Scrub it clean and saw the bottom off. Make a peephole, too.

A wood saw or hacksaw will cut a plastic bin.

16

DOORWAY TRICKS

Make yourself vanish from a doorway. You will need someone watching and a large cloth.

Find a cloth as wide as the doorway and longer than you. Try a table cloth, a sheet or towels pinned together.

Stand in the doorway holding the top of the cloth with both hands. Raise the cloth above your head so all of you is hidden except your hands.

Keep your hands where they are and move the rest of you sideways out of the doorway.

Drop the cloth and flash your arms out of sight at the same time. You won't do it the first time.

When you have practiced moving really fast you will seem to vanish. People in the room see you behind the cloth first – then nothing.

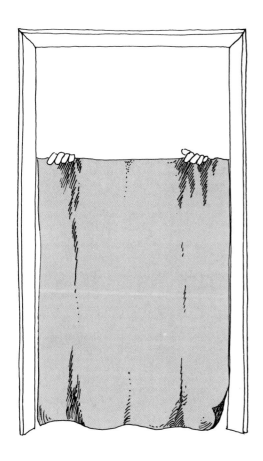
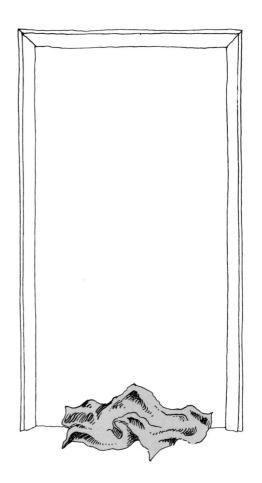

Stand in a doorway talking to people in a room. Stand so that just one side of you is showing – or just your head.

As you talk a hand comes from behind. It reaches over your head with grabbing fingers. Pretend not to notice – keep talking.

The hand gets slowly closer and closer to your head. Suddenly in the middle of a word it grabs you by the face. You are dragged out of sight screaming.

SPRING A SURPRISE

Hide in a huge cardboard cake at a feast.

You will need
2 boxes large enough to cover you
brown paper and tape
a sharp knife
a can of shaving soap

The smaller box must be wider than your shoulders.

You should be able to crouch inside the biggest box.

Cut a hole in the smaller box first. Make it large enough to let you spring through. Cover this hole in brown paper.

Now cut a hole in the larger box the same size. Tape the two boxes firmly together.

Decorate the cake with paper fringes and lots of shaving soap.

20

GROUP GAMES

Large groups of people can play games together. Here are two games for groups.

You need at least six people to play growing tag.

One person is chosen to start. That person tags someone who joins hands and races to tag another.

The group gradually grows until one person, the winner, is left.

A human chair chain can be used for emergency seating in damp places — or anytime you like.

Everyone gets into a circle with their shoulders touching.

Then everyone turns to the right and sits carefully down on the knees of the person behind. The person in front of you sits on you — so the circle is self-supporting.

THREE-LEGGED WALK

Make an extra leg for yourself with a straight stick dressed in a shoe, sock and trouser leg.

The stick should reach from the ground nearly to your elbow.

Stuff a sock with newspaper or old rags until it is foot-shaped. Poke the stick well down into the stuffed sock and tie it on tightly.

Dress the stick in a shoe and trousers – bundle up the trouser leg you don't need and tie it out of the way.

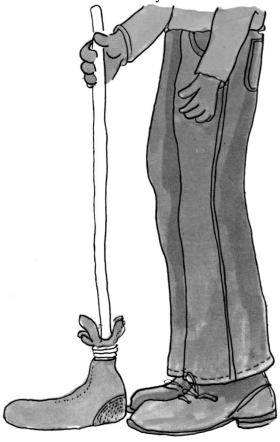

Now practise walking, holding the extra leg by your side. Outside feet work together best.

Once you can do a three-legged walk smoothly find a fairly long jacket that will hide the top of the stick. The hand holding the stick can go in a pocket.

Walk down the street as if you always had three legs – look surprised and cross if people stare.

HAIRY FACE

Get dressed one morning with all your clothes on back to front. Something with a collar looks best – and a hat.

Walk with your feet turned out, arms hanging down and your hands facing the other way.

Walk into breakfast backwards.

RACES

Ordinary races can be made more interesting by changing the rules.

Try running in pairs, back to back, and linked at your elbows.

Maybe each person could tie their knees together for another race. They must jump, waddle, hop or creep to the finishing line.

On hands and knees, roll a ball or a grape to a finishing line. Use your head to push the ball along.

Each person could have a sack to race in – or put each pair of people into a very large sack.

LAY AN EGG

You will need 2 hard-boiled eggs or pingpong balls.

Sit on an egg without anyone seeing you.

Pretend to force the other egg into your mouth and down your throat – but really keep it hidden in your hand.

While everyone is watching the look on your face, hide the egg in your pocket.

Give a huge swallow. Then make grunting noises and screw up your face so you look as if you are forcing the egg down.

After a while stop grunting. Stand up with a big smile of relief on your face – and there is the egg you laid.

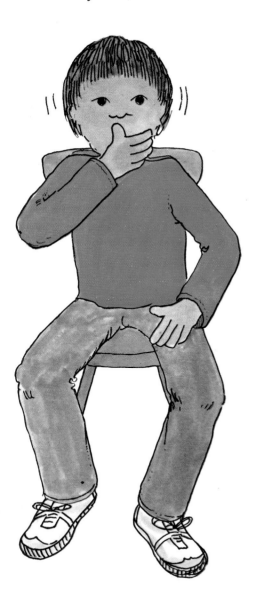

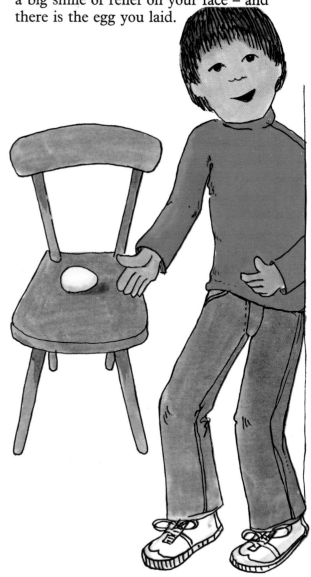

TAIL

A tail is a surprising thing to have. Make a long droopy one. Hang it through a hole cut in the seat of an old pair of jeans.

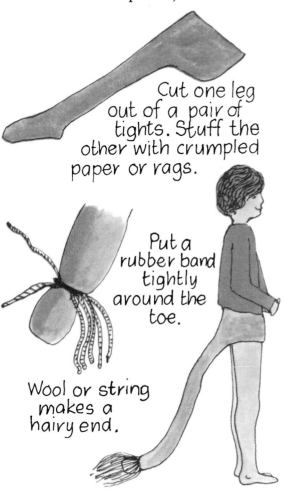

Cut one leg out of a pair of tights. Stuff the other with crumpled paper or rags.

Put a rubber band tightly around the toe.

Wool or string makes a hairy end.

Cut a hole in the trouser seam just big enough to push the tail through.

Practise walking and sitting in your tail so it becomes part of you.

SURPRISE SOUNDS

Trick and embarrass people with these simple noises.

This trick works best on someone wearing tight clothes. Get a small piece of cloth and cut a little way into it. This will make it easier to tear.

Now look out for someone about to squat down or bend over. As they bend, quickly and secretly make a loud ripping sound with the cloth. Watch how people madly check their clothes for rips.

Stop the conversation in a roomful of people with this rude noise.

Tightly hold the neck of a half blown-up balloon. Try to hide the balloon under your clothes.

Wait for someone to sit down and let a sudden splurt of air out of the balloon.

This trick also works well when someone sneezes, coughs or lifts something heavy.

HORROR IN THE DARK

Think of things that feel like parts of people.

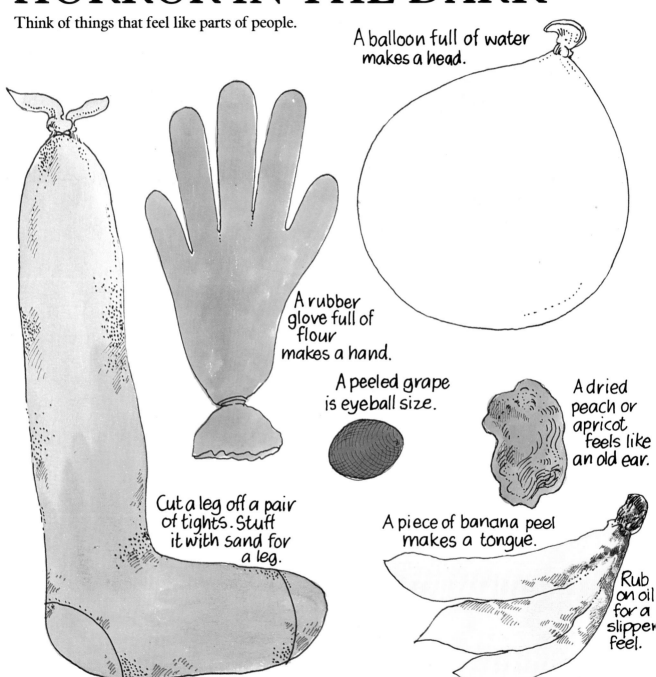

A balloon full of water makes a head.

A rubber glove full of flour makes a hand.

A peeled grape is eyeball size.

A dried peach or apricot feels like an old ear.

Cut a leg off a pair of tights. Stuff it with sand for a leg.

A piece of banana peel makes a tongue.

Rub on oil for a slipper feel.

Sit everyone in a row in the dark. Pass around the pieces as you tell a gruesome or ghostly story.

CHANGE YOUR SHAPE

Make yourself look wider all over. Wear boxes or pillows under your coat. Big shoes and baggy pants make larger legs.

Choose a coat a little smaller than you need and a tiny hat. This makes you look bigger still.

Padded cheeks and small lips painted on make a swollen face.

You can look shorter all over, too. You will need a friend to help.

Kneel down and tie a pair of rubber boots to your knees.

Put your hands on your shoulders and rubber gloves on your elbows for short arms.

Wear a large shirt with sleeves rolled up and a wide hat.

TAP SHOES

These have been used in many countries for hundreds of years. Tap dancing is a way of making as much sound as possible with dancing feet.

You can make a pair of shoes for tap dancing and teach yourself.

Metal hinges or metal bottle tops without the cork lining make good sounds.

Use a pair of shoes with very hard soles and no worn-down edges.

Screw the hinges in place or fasten the bottle tops with short nails like this.

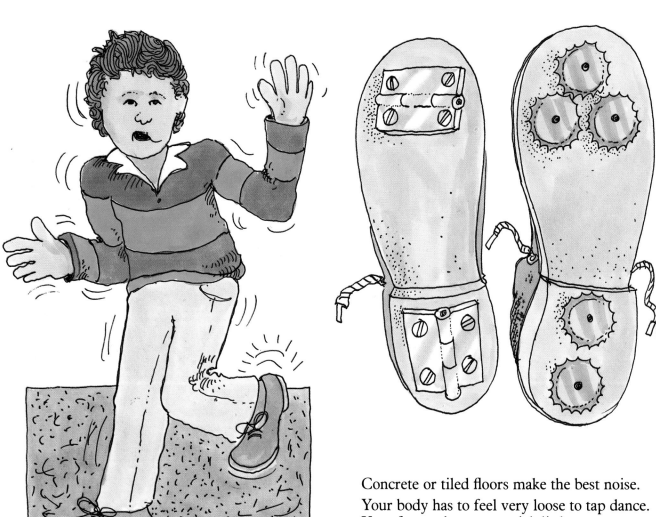

Concrete or tiled floors make the best noise.
Your body has to feel very loose to tap dance.
Your feet make many quick little movements.

Practise tapping your toe and then your heel with loose leg bones. When both feet can tap fast and easily, start dancing.

Invent your own steps. Dancing for a while each day will do much to improve your style.

Swing one foot after the other. Tap heel and toe with the swinging foot.

When you have a fast rhythm going, the tapping foot can make circles out to each side.

Add jumps and heel clicks when you can.

BOSOMS AND BOTTOMS

Here are some ways to make large bosoms and bottoms for wearing under your clothes.

They stay in place rather well so you can run and jump in them.

Old stretchy tights are the best things to use. You can stuff them with more tights or with soft rags.

Cut one leg off so you have a long tube.

Stuff it in two lumps and divide them with strings.

Tie them on – or use large safety pins.

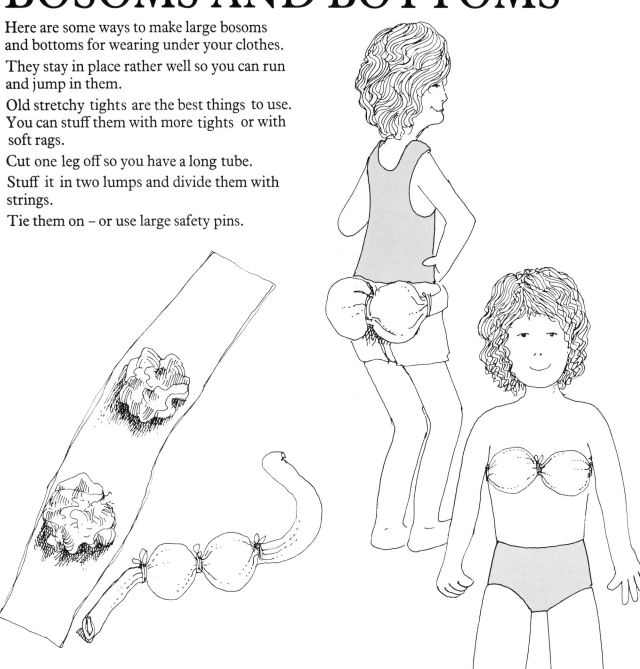

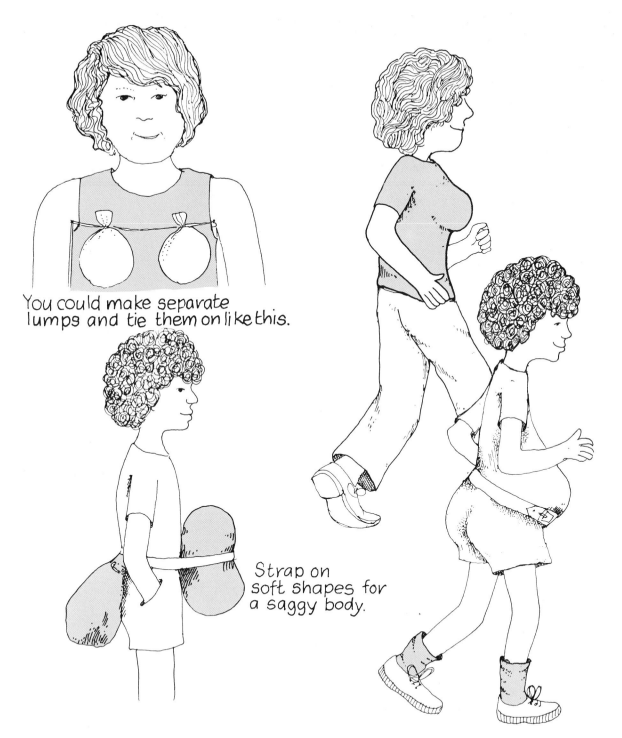

You could make separate lumps and tie them on like this.

Strap on soft shapes for a saggy body.

DEAD FINGER

Find a very small box – a matchbox is best.
Cut a hole in the bottom large enough for
your index finger to go through.

Whiten your finger a little and draw on
some bruises. Tuck cotton wool or tissues
around the finger. Dab on some tomato
sauce.

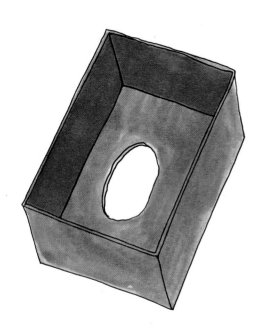

Shut the box as far as you can. Hold it in the palm of your hand so you can't see that your finger is the one in the box.

Make up a horrible story about finding a dead finger somewhere.

MIND READING

Some people seem to be able to send messages from their brain to another person's brain without signs or words. Messages have been sent over long distances between people who know each other well.

No one understands how this is done yet. The brain is still a puzzling thing. It may be that our minds have ways of signalling that most of us have forgotten how to use. A few people are very good at mind reading – but they can't explain it either.

Maybe you will find that you can sometimes mind read. Try it with someone you know well – a brother or a sister, a parent or a very good friend.

There are many ways to try mind reading. You could draw 5 or 6 pictures on cards. Choose clear shapes like a sun, boat, tree, cat, house and grapes.

The 5 cards on this page have been used to test mind readers. Scientists are trying to discover how the human brain works.

Copy the 5 signs on to cards. Make a set for each person and mark them clearly in strong black lines.

Find a quiet place to be. Lay each set of cards in a row in front of you and your partner. Have paper and a pencil ready to draw the sign.

Look at your row of cards and choose one in your mind. Think of it all the time.

There are lots of ways you could try to send the card across to your partner. Do whatever feels right for you.

Think of nothing else – this is the hardest part. One of you tries to have a blank mind while waiting for the message – and draws what comes. The sender tries to think of nothing but the card being sent.

Change over after a while. You might find your partner is better at sending than you are. See how many times you get the cards right. Sometimes you will and sometimes you won't.

Keep trying. One day you might find you are quite well tuned in to one another.

MEAN TRICK

Three of you could play this mean trick on someone.

The victim is blindfolded and seated on a small chair. A chair with rungs is best to keep the victim's feet off the ground.

Tell the blindfolded person to expect to be lifted to the ceiling.

Two of you stand on either side of the chair. The blindfolded person places both hands firmly on your shoulders.

Now grunt and puff as you seem to lift the chair. But just tilt and jiggle it as you slowly lower yourselves to the floor.

When you are as low as you can get, the victim will feel the ceiling is close. Your other friend can press a book on the victim's head.

Push the victim off the chair. The ground is much closer than expected.

MAKING THINGS

FORTUNE COOKIES

You can hide messages inside these cookies. Write a collection of messages on small pieces of paper.

Rice flour is best for fortune cookies. This lets them fold easily while they are warm – but be crisp when they are cool.

Get these things ready before you start.
4 eggs
$\frac{1}{2}$ a cup of melted butter or margarine
$\frac{1}{2}$ a cup of rice flour
$\frac{3}{4}$ of a cup of sugar
a pinch of salt
2 tablespoons of water
a bowl, an egg beater, a wooden spoon, a baking tray and an egg slice or spatula.

Set the oven at 350° or gas mark 4. Grease the baking tray well.

Separate the egg whites from the yolks.

You need the whites in the bowl.

The yolks can be used for something else.

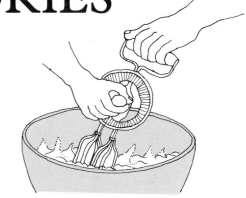

Beat the egg whites until they stand up in frothy points. This takes several minutes of hard work.

Stir in the rice flour, sugar and salt and beat the mixture well for another 2 minutes.

Add the melted butter and water and beat everything together until the mixture is like thin cream.

Put spoonfuls of the mixture on the baking tray. Leave plenty of room between each one.

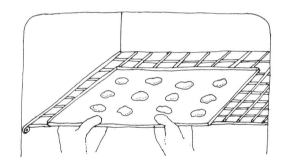

Bake them for 8 minutes, or until the edges are turning brown.

Lift off a hot cookie with the egg slice or spatula. Work as quickly as you can. The other cookies stay warm on the baking tray.

Put a message in the centre of each cookie and fold it up like this. If the cookies start to harden, you could put them back in the oven for a minute to soften again.

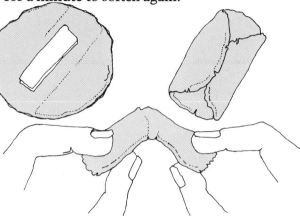

Store them when they are quite cool in an airtight jar.

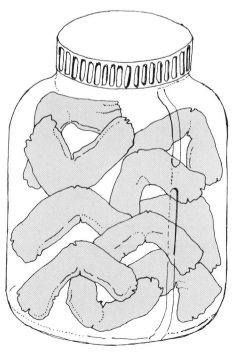

ALARM SYSTEM

This is an alarm for people who need something extra to wake them up in the morning. You could make one for a friend or for yourself. It should get the deepest sleeper moving.

You will need
a shoebox
lots of ping pong balls or balls of screwed up paper
an alarm clock with a large winder
string
a thin sheet of paper

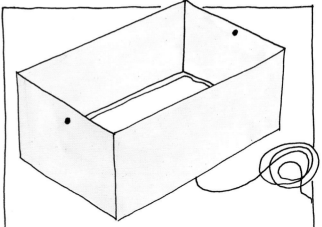

Punch a hole near the top at both ends of the box.

Now thread string through the holes in the box. Suspend it so that the paper-covered hole will be right over your head in bed.

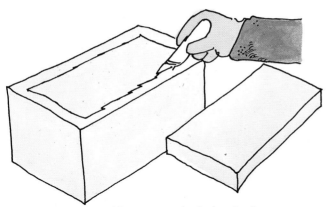

Use a sharp knife to cut a hole in the bottom of the shoebox. Leave a 2 cm rim all around.

Cut the sheet of paper so it is just longer and wider than the hole. Tape a long piece of string to the centre of one side. Put this into the box with the string on the outside.

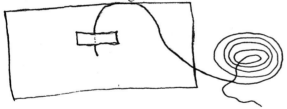

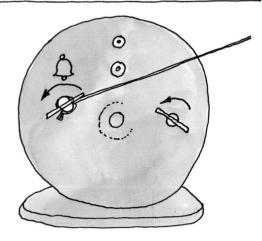

Set and wind the clock's alarm.

Tie the paper's string to the alarm winder on the back of your clock. Tie the tightest knot you can, and wind the string a few times in the direction of the clock's arrow.

Fill the box with the balls. Test the system till it works properly.

It works best if the clock is near the box. If the clock moves when it rings, stack books around it.

49

GLIDE BAR

A ride on a glide bar looks frightening and feels great. Collect exactly the right tools and materials as glide bars must be strong and safe.

First find a good wheel. A trolley wheel without its tyre or a fan-belt wheel from a car wrecker works well.

You will also need
metal pipe for a handle
a bolt with 4 washers and 2 nuts
a drill with bits the size of the handle and the bolt
wood, new rope and wood-working glue

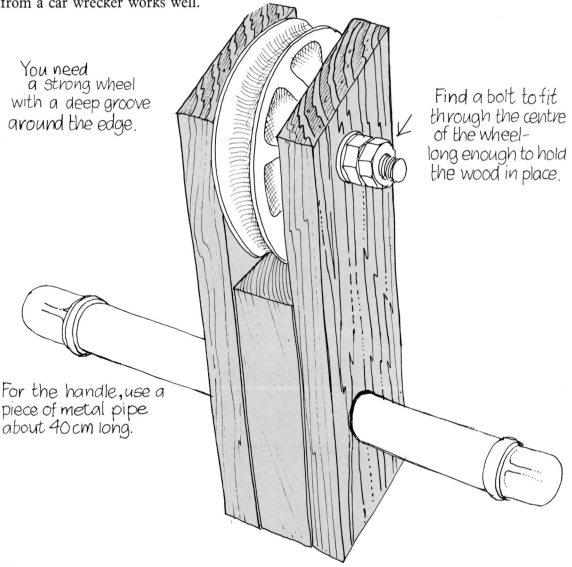

You need a strong wheel with a deep groove around the edge.

Find a bolt to fit through the centre of the wheel - long enough to hold the wood in place.

For the handle, use a piece of metal pipe about 40 cm long.

Use the drawing as a guide when you put the glide bar together.

Cut 3 pieces of wood – 2 the same size and the other shorter. Measure them against the wheel and the handle.

Drill holes for the bolt and for the handle. The handle goes through 3 thicknesses of wood. Leave room on the short piece for at least 5 cm above and below the handle.

Drill a hole through one piece first. Mark through that hole with a pencil on to each of the other pieces. Make the handle hole a tight fit.

Glue the short piece of wood between the other two. Use wood-working glue and give it plenty of time to dry.

Fit the handle through its hole. You could file the edges of the hole if it is too tight.

Put the wheel in place and thread the bolt through. A washer goes each side of the wood. Screw on the nuts tightly.

Thread the rope through between the wheel and the short piece of wood.

You also need at least 20 metres of strong rope to fit the groove in your wheel.

You need an open space for glide bar riding. Each end of the rope must be firmly tied to a strong support. Trees with large spreading branches, fire escapes and high fences make good supports.

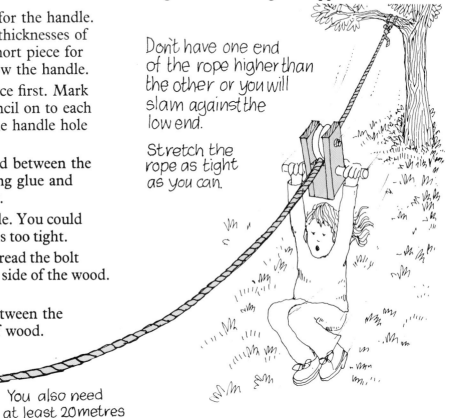

Don't have one end of the rope higher than the other or you will slam against the low end.

Stretch the rope as tight as you can.

Start with the ends of the rope tied higher than you can reach. Stand on a chair to tie them.

Test that your feet won't drag on the ground. Even if the rope looks tight, your weight will make it sag in the middle.

You and a few friends should hang on the rope to check your knots before you glide.

51

RAG PERSON

Make a rag person as big as you from your old clothes. Choose clothes that are not too thick and hard to sew.

You will need
a high-necked sweater
a stretchy sleeve from another sweater
a piece of rag for the face
a sweater or jacket for the top layer
a pair of trousers
a pair of socks
a pair of gloves
a large needle and strong thread
lots of soft rag for stuffing

The head is made from the extra sweater sleeve. Knot one end and stuff the sleeve into the tightest shape you can.

Stuff the socks next and sew the trouser bottoms around them. Now stuff the trousers tightly right down to the feet.

Stuff the gloves and sew the cuffs of the sweater around them. Now stuff the arms and body tightly into your shape.

Join your rag person together with lots of small stitches. Sew around the joins two or three times. Rag people burst easily.

Pummel the stuffing firmly into place around the neck and middle. Use extra stuffing if the neck is very floppy.

Sew on the face next. Then draw on eyes, a nose and a mouth with felt pens.

Dress the rag person in a top layer to hide the stitches.

WIND VANE

A wind vane tells you the direction the wind is blowing in. It has a sail that swings a pointer into the wind.

You will need
- a piece of wooden rod (dowel) about as long as your arm and 2 or 3 cm thick
- 2 flat boards for the base
- a fat thread spool of wood or plastic
- 1 very long nail (10 cm)
- some stiff plastic for the sail and pointer
- a clamp or a strong friend to hold the rod still while you saw and drill

Saw the 2 flat boards into points at both ends.

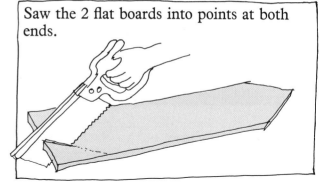

Nail them together to make the base. Mark north, south, east and west in large letters on both sides.

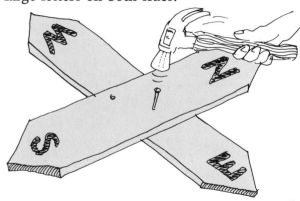

Cut out the sail and the pointer with a sharp knife.

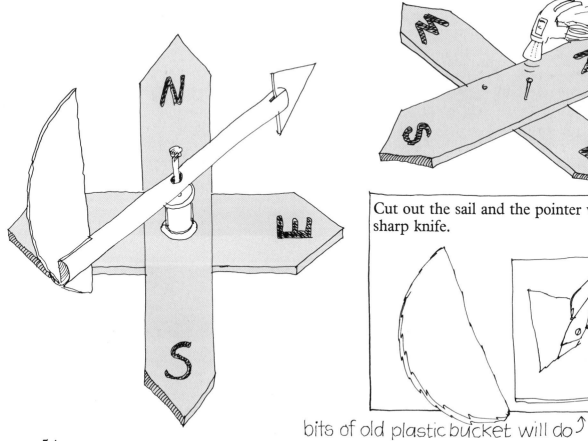

bits of old plastic bucket will do ↗

Cut notches in the wooden rod – a long one for the sail and a shorter one for the pointer. Test them to make sure they fit. If they are too loose fix them with glue.

a clamp is even better than a foot

Find the spot where the rod balances. Hang it from a piece of string and move the string until the rod hangs level. Mark this position with a pencil.

Drill a hole through the rod where you have marked. Use a bit in your drill that is a little fatter than the long nail. This lets the pointer swing free in the wind.

Drill through the center of the base but use a drill bit smaller than before for a tight fit.

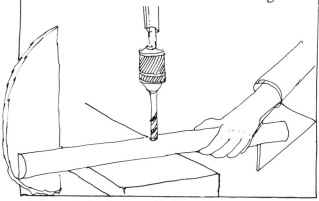

Thread the long nail through the rod and the spool then hammer it through the base.

Now find a windy place as high as you can get – a fence post or a wooden balcony rail works well. Make sure your north mark on the base faces north. Or find west as the sun goes down.

Now hammer the nail again to hold the wind vane in position.

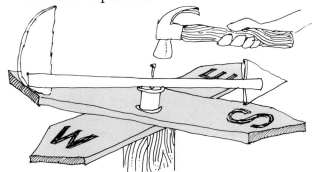

SPACE BOX

Ordinary things look strange when you can see only them. This happens when you look through a small hole in a piece of paper or down a long cardboard tube. Somehow things look clearer.

A space box is just a cardboard box with holes cut in it – but inside you can make a whole world. By looking through the small peephole with one eye everything else is shut out. The distance between things in the box looks much greater than it really is.

To make a space box find a strong cardboard box with a lid – a shoebox is about right. You will need scissors, tape, some paper to filter the light into the box, some magazines to cut up and felt pens and paper to draw your own things.

Make a small peephole in one end of the box. Then cut a square hole in the lid away from the peephole.

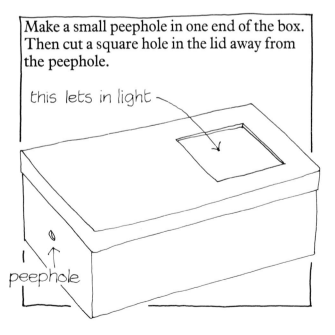

this lets in light

peephole

Cover the hole in the lid with paper to filter the light. Coloured tissue or cellophane casts a strange light. A square of silver foil can be used too. Punch a few holes in it to get sunlight in dark places.

tape the paper to the outside of the lid

Line the sides and the back of the box with something to make a background. Pictures of city streets or countryside work well. Silver foil and bright coloured fabric could make patterns.

Sand and pebbles can make the ground. Broken mirror can be water – or several pieces can reflect each other endlessly. Plastic tubes can change the shape of things seen through them.

Now fill your box with cutout figures, trees, shapes, buildings. Tape them in position – but check through the peephole each time to see where they should go. Everything looks different through the hole.

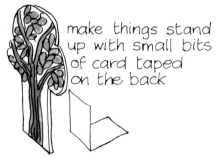

make things stand up with small bits of card taped on the back

Hang things on cotton from the roof to move gently in your space. Beads or small shiny things will sway and glitter.

Another hole in the far wall could be covered in cellophane to look like a stormy sky, a setting sun, or an underwater world.

A space box looks best when it is held under a strong light.

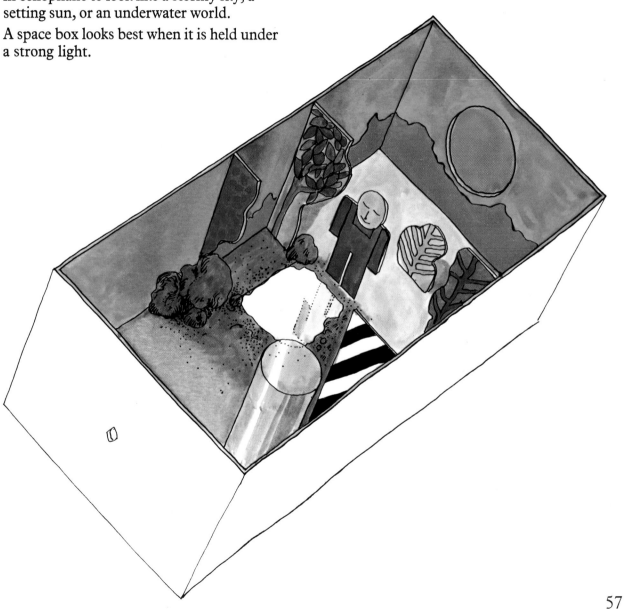

SOFT CHEESE

This is the easiest kind of cheese to make and has been made in many parts of the world for hundreds of years.

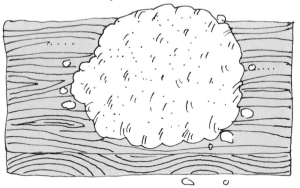

You will need
- 1 litre of milk
- 1 junket tablet
- 1 teaspoon of salt
- a coarse clean cloth (like an old tea towel)
- a saucepan, a spoon and two bowls

Put the milk in the saucepan over a low heat until it is lukewarm.

Crush the junket tablet in a bowl with the back of a spoon. Now dissolve the tablet in a few spoons of cold water.

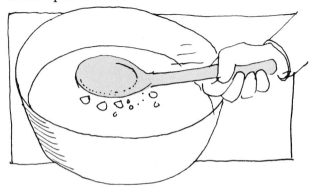

Pour the milk into the same bowl and stir.

Leave it to set in a warm place. In about 15 minutes the rennet from the tablet will clot the protein in the milk into a thick curd and a watery whey.

Cut the surface of the junket crisscross with the spoon and stir in the salt.

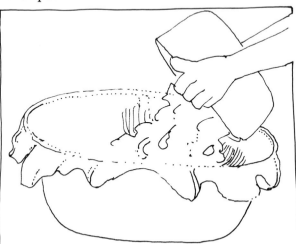

Now put your cloth over the other basin and pour the junket into it.

Tie the four corners of the cloth together and hang the bundle over a bowl to catch the drips of whey. A cool place (not the fridge) is best.

In half a day the cheese will be ready to eat–but you can leave it for 2 or 3 days if you want a stronger flavoured cheese.

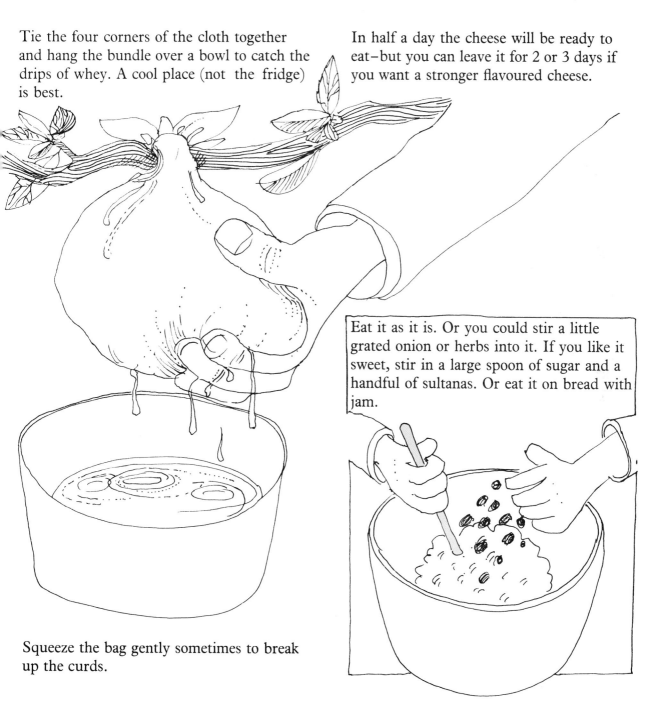

Eat it as it is. Or you could stir a little grated onion or herbs into it. If you like it sweet, stir in a large spoon of sugar and a handful of sultanas. Or eat it on bread with jam.

Squeeze the bag gently sometimes to break up the curds.

MUSICAL INSTRUMENT

You will need a large plastic bottle for the sound box. An orange juice bottle or a detergent bottle would do.

Other things to collect are

- a piece of wood about 5 cm wide and a bit longer than your arm
- some strong nylon fishing line
- 6 screw eyes

  a matchbox or a small block of wood

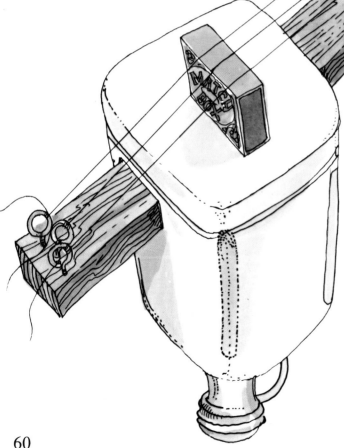

Cut a hole in each side of the bottle about 3cm from the bottom. This is to stick the piece of wood through - make it a very tight fit.

do this by drawing around the end of the wood - then cut just inside the mark with a sharp knife

With a hammer and a small nail make a shallow hole for each screw eye. Evenly space 3 at each end of the wood.

Tie 3 strands of fishing line tightly between the pairs of screw eyes. Allow plenty of extra length in the strands so you can knot them easily.

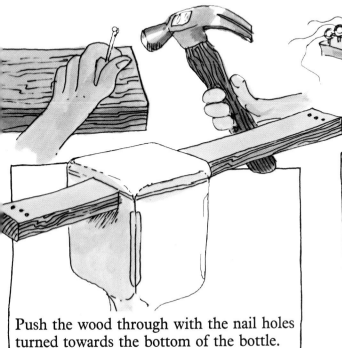

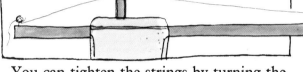

Slip the matchbox or block of wood under the strings on the end of the bottle.

Push the wood through with the nail holes turned towards the bottom of the bottle.

You can tighten the strings by turning the screw eyes.

When the strings are plucked the sound waves bounce around inside the empty bottle and make the sounds louder.

Screw the eyes into their holes.

61

AEOLIAN HARP

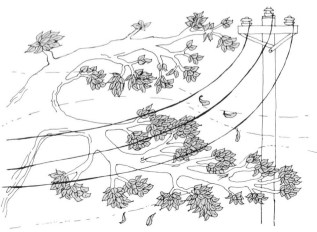

You will need
2 pieces of pine wood to fit your window
  (about 140 mm wide and 18 mm thick)
2 pieces of the same wood about 40 mm long
2 pieces of wooden rod about 15 mm thick
12 large screw eyes, some thin 50 mm nails
1 set of guitar strings, a hammer, a drill and
a drill bit the same size as the screw eyes

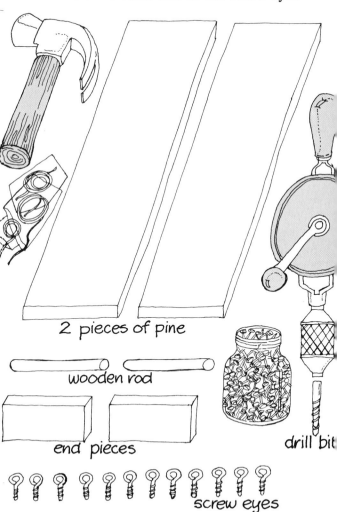

2 pieces of pine

wooden rod

end pieces

drill bit

screw eyes

People don't give the wind much thought most of the time. It has to be really whistling through the telephone wires or blowing us off balance to be noticed.

Here is a way to make an aeolian harp to remind you of the wind. This is an ancient instrument that plays music when the wind blows. Strange soft sounds can be heard as the strings vibrate.

People long ago thought there was something magical about the aeolian harp. Certainly the sound it makes seems to come from nowhere.

The best place for catching even the gentlest breeze is in the bottom of a partly open window. You could try the harp in a tree or on a wall outside, too. Choose a quiet place or the music could be drowned out.

If your harp is to go in a window, make it an exact fit. That way all the wind is funnelled through the harp. Measure the inside of the window frame.

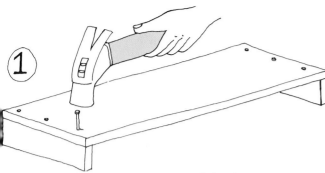

① Nail the end pieces to one of the long boards.

② Mark 2 lines about 5 cm from the ends and drill holes for the screw eyes.

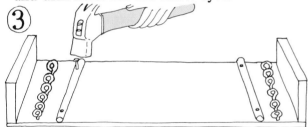

③ Screw in the screw eyes. Nail the wooden rods about 5 cm from them.

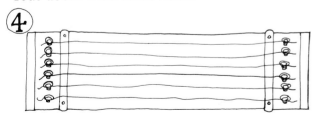

④ Tie the guitar strings to the screw eyes in order of thickness.

Fasten the top in place with one nail. It swivels so you can tune the strings easily.

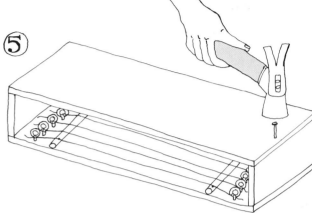

⑤

To tune your harp, start with the thinnest string. Turn the screw eyes until the string sounds a low note when you pluck it.

Then tighten the other strings until they make the same note. The thick strings will be tighter than the thin strings.

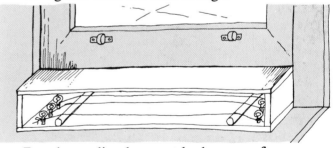

Put the aeolian harp at the bottom of an open window. Shut the window to hold the harp in place. Or fasten it firmly in a tree.

Wait for the wind to blow. At first you will hear a gentle hum. Listen as the wailing sounds start to build up as the strings vibrate. The sound will come and go with the wind.

FOUR-POSTER BED

Modern beds are not the private places old beds were.

Make 4 long posts for your bed from broom handles or scrap wood.

Tie the posts on – or nails won't hurt an old bed.

A canopy roof and walls could be a large sheet. Crepe paper and cut-out stars and shapes could be pinned to it.

You could make a four-poster bed from newspaper tubes.

You will need lots of newspaper, tape and string.

Make many strong newspaper tubes like this.
Roll six sheets of paper tightly into tubes.

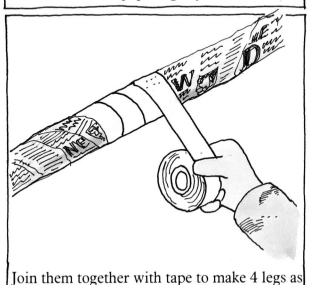

Join them together with tape to make 4 legs as tall as you need.

Tie them to the legs of your bed. If your bed has no legs, a long piece of fat elastic could hold the tubes in place.

Now measure the distance between the legs for the top of the frame.

Make enough tubes to fill the gaps. They should be a little longer than the sides. Join the tubes with tape and bend over the ends like this.

You can now slot the frame together.

BOTTLE ISLAND

You and your friends can make a floating island from plastic bottles and onion bags.

Onion bags won't rot and are easy to sew. Use one onion bag inside another for extra strength.

You need lots of plastic bottles with screw-on lids to keep water out and air in.

Eight double onion bags filled with bottles makes an island big enough for 2 people. Ten people could work together to fill 20 double bags.

Use plastic string and a large needle to sew up the openings in the bags.

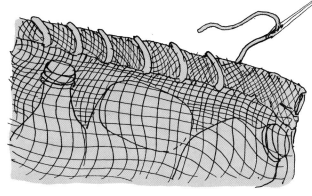

When you have enough bagfuls sew them all together.

Take your time and use firm knots to start and finish – or your island will collapse under rough treatment.

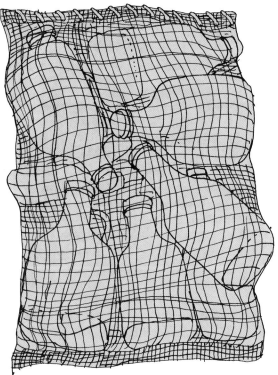

Screw the lids on the bottles tightly. Then pack them into each double onion bag.

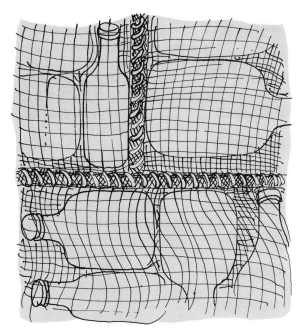

A bottle island can be as large as you like.
It can carry a floor of planks and a
shelter, too.

PERFORMING BOX

This is a small stage which stands out in a crowd. People used to take puppet shows to the beach long ago.

You could do a talking head show, a glove puppet show or use cut-outs on long sticks.

Make a box a good deal taller than you. You stand in it and reach up to the stage. If you are the performance, make a shorter box so just your head can be seen.

Use large cardboard cartons wider than you. Collect 4 or 5 that are almost the same shape.

Cut the sides out of the cartons. Leave rims for taping together. Bricks or large stones on the bottom rims stop the box blowing over.

You will need to plan your show carefully if people are going to pay for it.

A group of you could work together.

Practise your act until it is just right. Check if your voice can be heard through the box from a long way off.

Announce when the show is going to start. Maybe one of you could move among the crowd with a loud hailer and an odd looking hat.

This person gets the crowd to sit down in front of the box, collects the money, and asks for silence.

The show can then begin.

TROLLEY

This is a perfect present for people whose legs don't work – or for anyone else who would enjoy skidding around on it.

You will need
3 pieces of 50 mm x 50 mm timber each 50 cm long
1 piece of 50 mm x 25 mm timber 60 cm long
1 piece of 50 mm x 25 mm timber 25 cm long
a sheet of thick plywood
4 ball castors
lots of 50 mm flat-headed nails
a hammer, a coping saw, a drill,
a G-clamp, sandpaper and a pencil

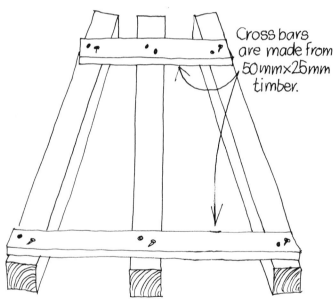

Cross bars are made from 50 mm x 25 mm timber.

A trolley must be very strong so make it carefully.

Set the timber out like this to make the trolley frame. Use 2 nails in each joint to hold it together firmly.

Lie the frame on the plywood sheet with the wide end about 3 cm from one edge.

Draw straight lines 3 cm from each sloping side of the frame.

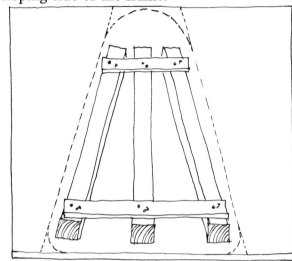

Then draw curving lines to make a round-cornered triangle.

Saw along the lines you have drawn.

Hold the plywood steady with a clamp as you saw.

Nail the plywood shape to the frame.

Drill holes for the castors in the cross bars. Use a drill bit the same size as the screw-in rod on the castors.

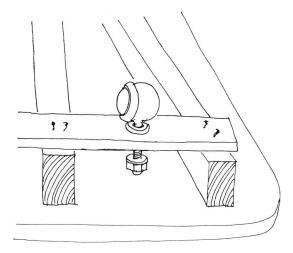

Two castors go at the wide end of the frame. Place them as far apart as you can. The other castors go at the front.

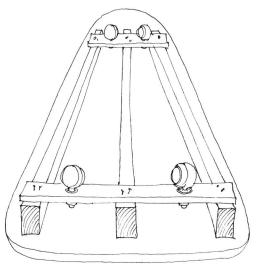

You can add things to the trolley to suit the person you are making it for.

A cushion makes the trolley soft to lie on. A hole can be drilled in the front and a rope threaded through for towing the trolley up hills. Use extra castors if the person who will ride on it is very heavy.

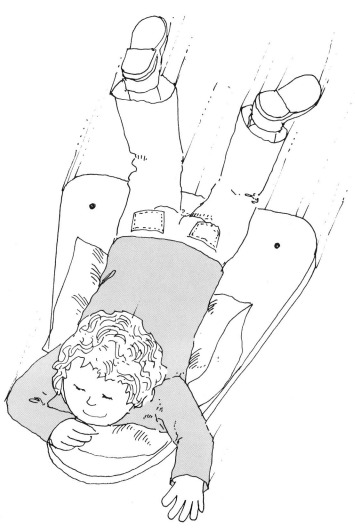

CLOAK

This is a way to make a swirling cloak from a large square of material. A table cloth works well.

Lay your square flat and fold it in half then in half again. Draw a large curve for the hem and a small curve for the neck hole.

Clear a large space on the floor to work on. Open out the circle and lie it flat. Now cut a straight slit from the outside in to the neck hole.

Then cut along your lines. Four thicknesses are hard to cut through so cut the top layer first for a pattern.

Neat edges aren't necessary for most cloaks, but they will help a special cloak last longer. Use an iron to press the neck edge over.

Fold the bottom hem and front edges over and press them, too. Keep them flat with lots of pins.

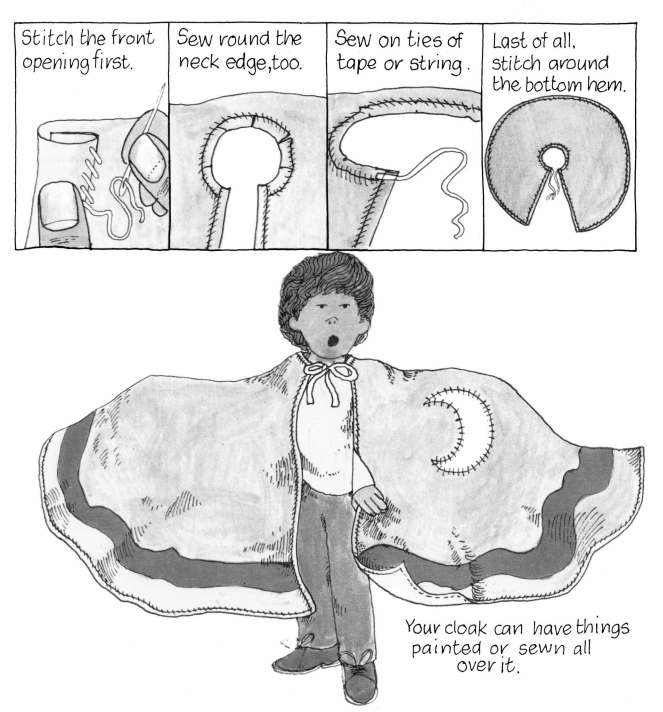

Stitch the front opening first.

Sew round the neck edge, too.

Sew on ties of tape or string.

Last of all, stitch around the bottom hem.

Your cloak can have things painted or sewn all over it.

BREAD

This is one of the oldest foods and one of the best things to make. It is not as hard as it sounds.

Bread takes about 3 hours from start to finish – but you can do other things while it rises.

To make 1 loaf you will need

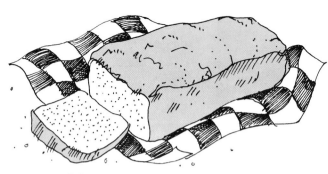

- 3 cups of flour – this can be plain, wholemeal, or a mixture of both
- 1 tablespoon of fresh yeast or 2 teaspoons of dried yeast
- 1 cup of warm water – not hot
- 1 teaspoon of sugar
- 1 teaspoon of salt

Get these things ready as well.

YEAST

Yeast is the magic ingredient in bread which makes it rise and feel light. Yeast is a plant. It needs warmth, food – sugar and flour – and water to grow.

You can use fresh yeast which looks like putty, or dried yeast from a packet.

There are 2 very important things to do when you are making bread. First knead the dough for a long time to mix the yeast through. Then have a warm place to leave it to rise – in the sun or by a warm stove perhaps.

Kneading is a special way of mixing dough with your hands. It is hard work. The dough will slowly change from a sticky mess into a smooth springy lump. Keep 1 cup of the flour you need for sprinkling on your hands and the dough while you work.

large bowl

small bowl

cup

clean cloth

floury board

baking tin rubbed with butter or oil

1 yeast

mix yeast with ½ a cup of warm water and a spoon of sugar

2 put **2** cups of flour and a spoon of salt into bowl

make a well with your fist

3 pour in yeast and sprinkle with flour

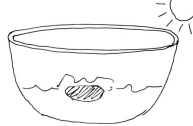

leave in a warm place until the yeast froths

4 pour in ½ a cup of warm water

mix very well with floury hands into a smooth lump

5 cover with cloth and leave in a warm place

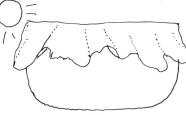

after about **45** minutes the dough will be twice as big

6 turn dough on to a floury board

with very floury hands knead the dough until your wrists ache - then some more

7 turn the oven on to **450** degrees or gas mark **8** to heat up

shape the dough into a loaf in the tin - leave it to rise to the top for another **45** minutes

8 put the loaf in the oven

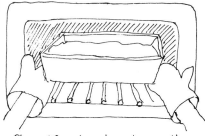

after **10** minutes turn the oven down to **350** degrees or gas mark **4**

9 have a look after **45** minutes

the loaf is cooked when it shakes out of the tin and sounds hollow when you tap it.

PANTOMIME HORSE

A pantomime horse looks strangely real on the stage or walking down the street.

You and a friend can be a horse together. One of you bends over and holds on to the waist of the other standing in front.

For the horse's body you will need a large square of cloth.

Cut a slit in it long enough to go round the middle of the person standing in front. Safety pins help you get a perfect fit.

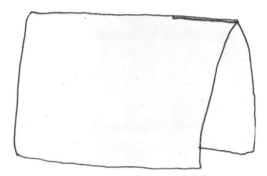

Use something that nobody wants and paint it in horse colours.

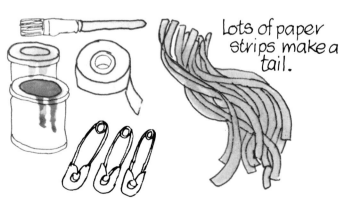

Lots of paper strips make a tail.

Two strong supermarket paper bags make the horse's head. Another bag makes ears, a mane and a tail.

This bag goes on your head.

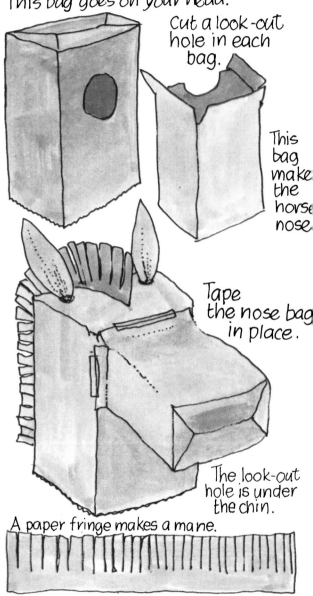

Cut a look-out hole in each bag.

This bag makes the horse nose.

Tape the nose bag in place.

The look-out hole is under the chin.

A paper fringe makes a mane.

76

Paint the head to match the body.
You should wear horse-coloured trousers
and shoes.

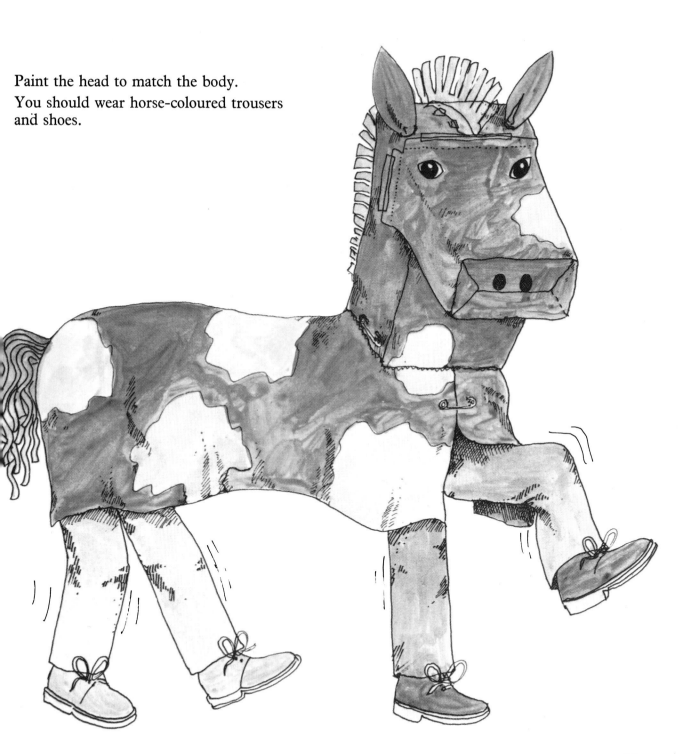

BURGLAR ALARM

Make a simple alarm system to frighten unwanted people from your door. When an invisible wire is tripped it flicks a switch to a blaring radio.

You will need
a transistor radio
about 5 metres of twin cord speaker wire
2 spring pegs
fishing line
a small thin piece of card
a nail and some strong tape

Split the wire at both ends into two 15 cm strands. Use a sharp knife to strip off the plastic coating 4 cm from the end of each strand.

Push this between the contact points of 2 batteries and tape the wires down to keep them apart. If your radio takes only one battery have the card between a terminal and the battery.

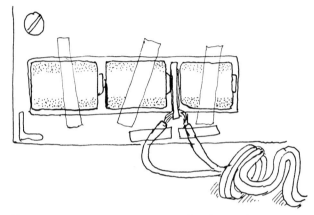

Put some more tape across the batteries so they won't fall out.

Take the circuit breaker out while you work on the wires.

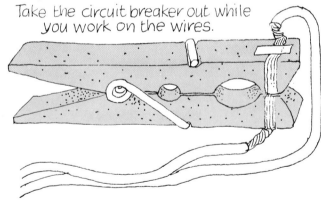

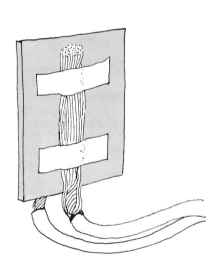

Make a circuit breaker for the radio. Cut out a 2 cm square of card. Attach a bare strand to each side of the card. Hold them in place with two small strips of tape across the top and bottom.

At the other end of the wire wind the bare end of a strand around the top half of a peg. Wind the other strand around the lower half of the same peg. Hold the wires in place with some tape on the outside

Now you need to make a triggering device to flick the switch.

Fix the wired peg to the door jamb with the nail. Have it just a little way from the floor.

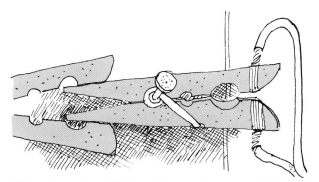

Tie a length of fishing line to the end of the other peg. Clip this peg on to the end of the switch peg to hold it open.

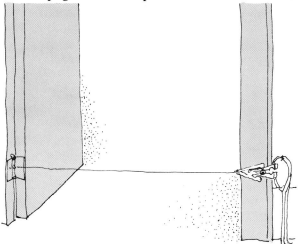

Stretch the fishing line across the doorway and tie it to a hinge. Test that the switch snaps shut when the fishing line is tripped. Make sure the switch wires press together.

Put your radio in a casual place and tape down the wire leading to the peg. Try to make it as invisible as you can.

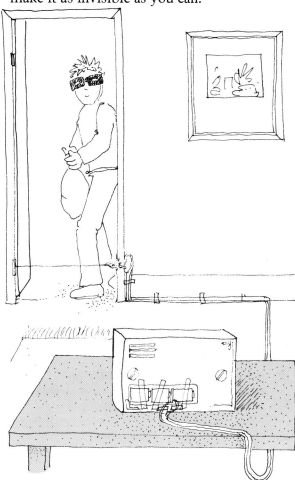

Have the radio switched on and set as loud as it will go. Give your alarm system a final test. If it doesn't work check that all the connections are firm.

You could rig up this alarm on a tape recorder too. Put your message to the burglar on a cassette and have it ready to play.

MESSAGE TRACK

Messages can be sent by string in a straight line between two places. Quite long distances can be covered if nothing is in the way.

You will need a pulley for each end, nails or cuphooks and a large ball of strong string. Don't use string with lots of knots in it or the pulleys won't work smoothly.

Your message carrier can be a clothes peg with a spring. You could also make a box to hold things as well as messages.

Cuphooks can hold the pulleys. Screw them to something firm at each end of the track. A window frame or branch works well.

You need a length of string from one pulley to the other and back again. Make a strong knot that will go through the pulley.

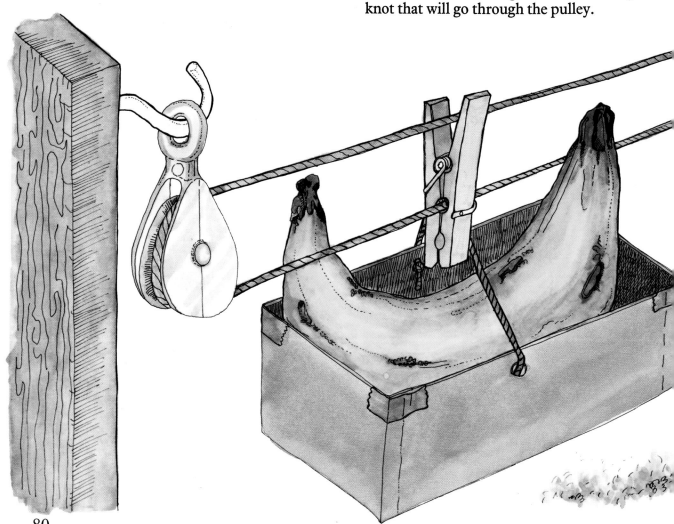

You pull on one string to bring the message to you and on the other to send it to someone at the other end.

ICE CREAM

Your own ice cream is twice as good as shop ice cream.

You will need
- 2 eggs
- ½ a cup of cream
- 2 tablespoons of icing sugar

First separate the egg yolks from the egg whites. This is rather hard to do. You want the yolks in a cup and the whites in a mixing bowl.

Crack the egg on the edge of the bowl and gently break the shell into 2 halves with your fingers.

Tip the yolk carefully from one shell half to the other, and back again. The white dribbles down into the bowl.

Beat the egg whites with an egg beater until they make a thick white froth.

In another bowl beat the cream until it is thick. Two people could share the beating.

Tip the cream into the egg whites and mix them together well.

5

Put the egg yolks into the empty bowl and tip in the sugar. Stir into a smooth mixture.

6 Mix everything together. Flavour the ice cream now if you like. Try peanut butter or small pieces of fruit.

7 Pour the mixture into a small cake tin or ice tray and put it in the freezer.

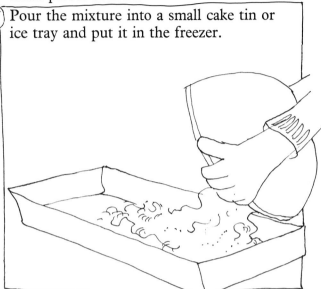

The ice cream will take an hour or so to freeze hard.

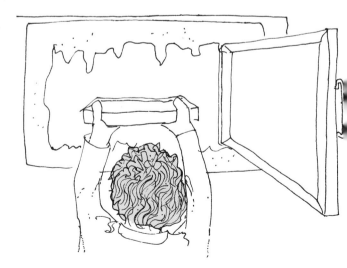

CREAM BUN

Split a bun or a bread roll. Spread it with jam
or jelly and fill it with cream. Add icing and a
cherry on top for special feasts.

CHIP BUTTY

This is an old name for a chip sandwich.

Use hot
chips and
add
tomato
sauce
if you
like.

EXPLORING

LONG DISTANCE RIDING

You can go a long way on a bike. You can keep going for hours if you are used to riding and go at a steady pace to keep your strength up. In traffic you will have to travel slowly, but if the roads you choose are fairly quiet with not too many hills you will be able to cover about 15 kilometres in an hour.

If you plan a long ride work out on a map which would be the quietest roads to take. Bikes aren't allowed on freeways, and roads with several lanes of traffic are best kept away from.

In the country cars usually go much faster than they do in cities. It is also hard to tell how fast a car is moving. Be on the lookout all the time.

Take your tools with you and a puncture repair kit. If you are going a long way take some spare nuts too.

You get very hot riding for hours so wear lightweight clothes. A waterproof jacket or a hat if it is hot can be carried rolled up in a saddlebag.

It is a good idea to take a supply of quick energy food in your pack too. Chocolate and apples are great revivers. Take a bottle of water if you are out in the wilds.

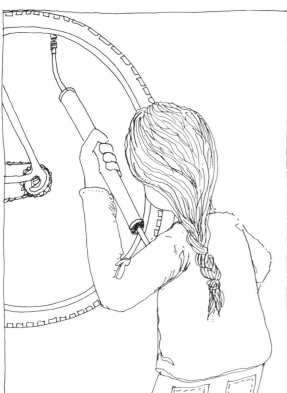

Check your bike over before you set off. Oil all the moving parts, pump up the tyres, and tighten the nuts on the wheel hubs, seat and handlebars. Make sure your brakes are working well.

86

A camping tour with a few friends is one of the best things to do on bicycles. It takes a lot of planning but everything you would need for days can be packed on a bike.

bikes are hard to steer
if the load is not
balanced – keep packs
low down

COUNTRY SHOW

A country-style show or fair needs lots of space. There will be creatures around that will need to be kept apart.

Lots of planning is needed too. Start several weeks ahead.

This kind of show is a competition. People bring their animals, plants, sewing, carpentry and cooking. Judges pick the best.

Let everyone in the neighbourhood know about the show. Make a list of the things they can enter.

People pay to enter their things in the show. Choose someone to be a judge for each section. Make decorated cards for the winners – or blue paper ribbons.

COUNTRY SHOW
AT THE PARK
SATURDAY 11am.
PRIZES FOR:
The ugliest cat.
The dog most like its owner.
The fastest billy cart.
The fanciest hat.
The best home-grown vegetables.
The most talkative bird.

1st 2nd 3rd

THE UGLIEST CAT

Have a place ready for each section. Flowers, vegetables and food will need tables. Have lots of signs on pegs in the ground to tell people where to take their entries.

Side-shows earn extra money and keep people busy while the judging is done. Invent your own. Three throws at a pile of cans works well.

KEEPING WARM

Never go off into the wilderness in very cold weather. People die that way.

Don't go camping or for a long walk with too few clothes – even in mild weather. It is usually much colder than you expect. Know how to look after yourself.

Bodies make their own heat as we breathe and eat. To keep warm in the open this heat must be kept in a layer of air near our skin.

Damp skin loses its warmth 20 times as quickly as dry skin. Wind blowing on damp clothes and skin cools them much faster than still air.

Not only rain makes you wet. If you wear too many tight clothes you will sweat inside them.

So the best way to keep warm and dry is to wear loose layers of clothes with a windproof and waterproof covering outside.

Food makes body warmth so eat plenty outdoors in the cold. Hot drinks warm you quickly – but you will need a thermos flask or billy can and matches.

If you are caught in the cold without enough clothes, trap a layer of warm air next to your body. Stuff your clothes with dry grass or bracken fern or newspaper.

The night is the coldest time. Even if it seems quite warm when you go to sleep you can wake up freezing just before dawn.

A thick sleeping bag is the best thing to sleep in. If the weather is freezing 2 people in one bag will keep each other warm.

clothes for cold weather

woollen hat to pull over cold ears

waterproof jacket with a hood

several loose layers underneath

gloves

warm pants

thick woollen socks

boots big enough to let your toes wriggle – they keep warmer that way

Remember that cold comes up from underneath as well as down from above. Stuff a thick layer of bracken fern or grass under your ground sheet to keep really warm.

You can get very sick from the cold and hardly notice what is happening to you. Don't take any chances. Never walk too far in cold weather. Stop long before you get tired.

If you are caught a long way from home and start to shiver and stumble, stop and take shelter until you warm up. Eat something and have a hot drink if you can. In the snow the quickest shelter may be a trench. You must get out of the wind.

BROODER

Newly hatched ducklings and chickens must live in a warm brooder box before going into an outside pen.

Chickens need to stay in the brooder until they are 4 or 5 weeks old. Ducklings are stronger and can go out in fine weather when they are 2 weeks old.

You can warm the brooder with a 40 watt light bulb inside a clay flower pot.

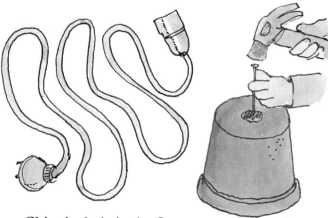

Chip the hole in the flower pot with an old chisel or a large nail. Make it large enough to fit the bulb holder.

Many pet shops and markets have very young chickens and ducklings for sale.

It's best not to decide in a hurry that you want to buy some. You must have things ready before taking such small creatures home.

Newly hatched ducklings and chickens are meant to be sheltered by the warmth of their mothers' bodies. Away from there they can easily die from cold. Even gentle hands can hurt their soft bones.

Once they are chilled or tired or hurt almost nothing can save them.

Remember too, that they are going to grow into large birds needing space and lots of looking after.

Decide how and where poultry can live in your garden. Think about the food they will need. Get advice from a poultry farm about this.

You will need a bulb holder on the end of a long cord. A plug goes on the other end.

Make a brooder out of 2 wooden boxes joined together. The floor should be covered in clean sand and newspaper.

Cover the brooder with loose boards. These can be taken off as the chickens or ducklings get older and stronger.

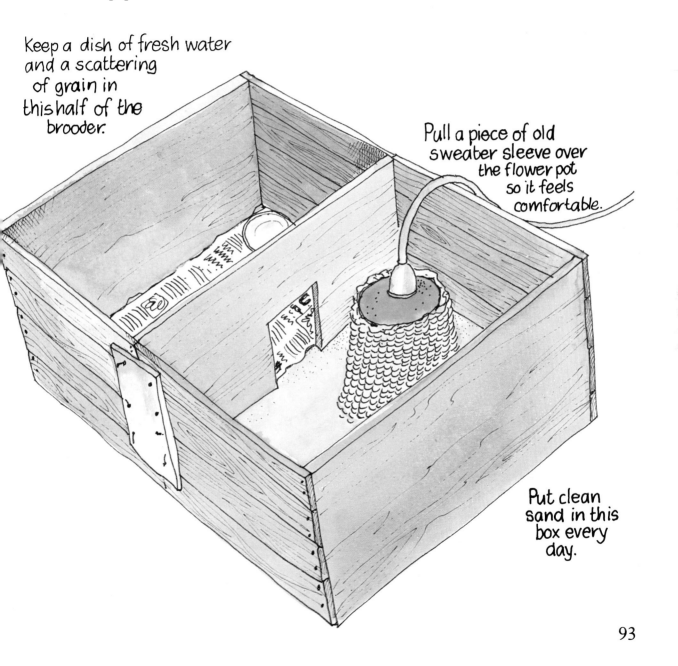

Keep a dish of fresh water and a scattering of grain in this half of the brooder.

Pull a piece of old sweater sleeve over the flower pot so it feels comfortable.

Put clean sand in this box every day.

WORM FARM

People who like fishing need bait. Earthworms make some of the best bait for fresh-water fish.

Start a worm farm in large buckets. If all goes well you will have many hundreds of worms to sell after 12 weeks.

You will need
2 old buckets
earth
lots of garden worms
a packet of dry-meal dog food

Make plenty of small drainage holes all over the sides and bottoms of the buckets. Use a hammer and a thin nail.

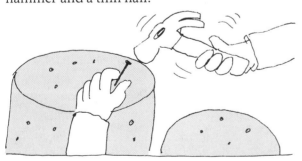

Fill a bucket with rich crumbly garden earth. Add a cup of dog food and mix it in well.

Sprinkle the earth with water until it is moist but not soggy.

Collect about 25 worms. To find them, dig deep with a spade in a healthy garden or compost heap. Put them on top of the earth-filled bucket. They will burrow out of sight.

Stand the bucket on bricks in a trough of water. Ants eat worms – the water keeps them out. Rats and mice eat worms too. Cover the bucket with a piece of fine wire mesh if you are worried.

Start a crop of worms in the second bucket after about a month. This will give you a steady supply.

Check the worm farm once a week to see if it is still moist. Water it gently. Too much water is worse than too little.

Every 3 weeks take about 10 cm of earth from the top of the buckets. Mix this earth with ½ a cup of dog food.

Tip the rest of earth out of the buckets. Put fresh food mixture in the bottom of each bucket. Now replace all the earth.

This is a good time to check how the farm is going. If the earth is muddy or mouldy you have been adding too much water or food.

You should see young worms after 6-8 weeks. These will be big enough to sell after 12 weeks.

Collect empty tin cans to sell the worms in. Damp moss in the cans keep the worms fit for fishing. You could put 20 worms in each can, maybe.

Work out how much money the farm costs. You might have to buy buckets. The dog food will cost money too. Work out how much you should charge for the worms.

Set up a worm stall near a road that leads to a well-known fishing place.

DIRTY AIR

There have always been things floating in the air for us to breathe – pollen from plants, dust, sand, smoke from bushfires and fireplaces.

Our noses are lined with small damp hairs to trap these things and to keep them out of our lungs. But we can't filter out city air any more.

Have a close look at some of the things cars and trucks put into the air.

Make a filter for the exhaust pipe of a car or truck. A white sock or a handkerchief works best. Tie the filter over the exhaust pipe.

Choose a car that has been parked for a while so the exhaust pipe has cooled.

Ask the driver to turn on the engine for one minute.

When the engine stops take off the filter carefully – the exhaust pipe will be hot.

Look inside the filter. What you see is only part of what we breathe in – the rest is invisible.

One of the very worst air polluters is invisible. This is sulphur dioxide gas which kills plants, gives people bronchitis and eats away at buildings.

If you have two silver-plated spoons you can test for this gas.

Polish both the spoons until they are shiny clean.

Find a place to hang one spoon where there is heavy traffic. Keep the other spoon inside.

Compare the spoons after a week. If your area has sulphur dioxide gas in the air, the outside spoon will be grey and tarnished.

FRUIT

You can measure the amount of grit in the air in different places.

Cut a piece of white cardboard into squares. Cover one side of each square with a thin coating of Vaseline.

Pin up one square in your room. Others could go near a busy street corner, or maybe up a tree in a city park.

Hang a square on each side of the tree to see where the grit comes from.

If you know a smoking factory, nail a square nearby. The people in charge might take some notice if you can show them the grit they cause.

The grit sticks to the Vaseline. Check the cards at the same time next day to see which places have the dirtiest air.

MUSHROOMS

These are some of the most
mysterious things of all to grow.

If you have trouble collecting the things
you need, look in the telephone book for
mushroom growers in your area.

3 buckets of chicken or horse manure

1 or 2 waxed cardboard or wooden boxes

mushroom spawn

1 bottle or block of mushroom spawn

1 bucket of straw

Heap the manure and straw together and
mix it with a fork. If the pile is out in the
open cover it with a sack or plastic sheet.

make a moist mixture

After a few days the pile will feel hot.
Turn it over and if it has dried out water
it lightly. Do this every few days for
about 3 weeks.

The manure mixture is ready when it is brown and crumbly. Pack it firmly into the boxes so they are almost filled.

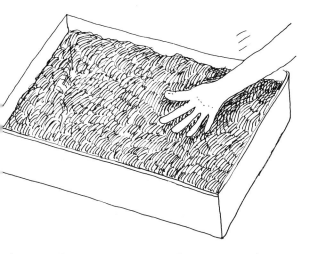

Crumble the mushroom spawn and press it into the surface of the manure.

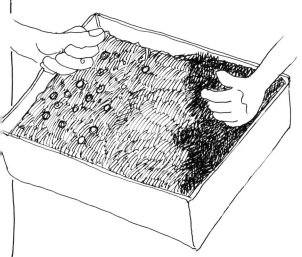

Fill the boxes right up now by covering the manure with a layer of damp garden soil.

Put the boxes in a sheltered place where there are no drafts – under the house, or in a cupboard or shed.

Keep the mushroom beds damp but not wet. Too much water will kill them.

If the weather is not too cold you will see tiny white dots after about 6 weeks. One week later the first mushrooms will be big enough to eat. More and more will appear for several months.

ROSE-COLOURED SPECTACLES

Make yourself a pair of rose-coloured spectacles and wear them for a while. This gives you a new look at things and people around you.

Everything is changed by seeing them through a colour – they won't all be pink.

You will need some red or pink cellophane and some old spectacles you can take the glass out of. Or make a pair of spectacles out of stiff card.

Cover the eye holes with cellophane stuck on with tape. Try more than one layer if your paper is light pink.

Use blue or green spectacles too. The world won't look so cheerful.

you'll need 2 of these

trace these shapes on to a card and cut them out

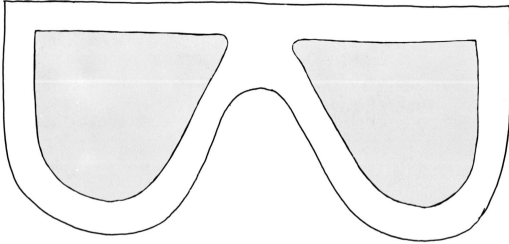

join the spectacles together with tape

DIRTY WATER

The world's water is getting dirtier and dirtier. Fish and birds and animals and people need water to survive.

You can find out how clean a freshwater creek or river is by looking at the small creatures that live there.

A few things can live in very dirty water. Others die if their water changes in any way.

You will need a small net. Make one from thin wire and a piece of nylon stocking.

Cut the stocking off above the knee and tie a tight knot in the narrow end.

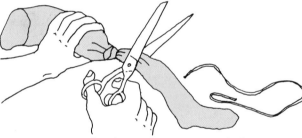

Thread the wire in and out around the top. The two ends of the wire are twisted around a long stick to make a handle.

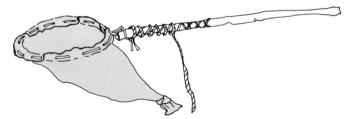

Find a collecting dish with a white bottom. This shows up the tiny creatures you will find.

Choose a shallow place on the water's edge away from steep, slippery or crumbling banks.

Fill your dish with the clearest water you can see.

Now scoop your net through any weeds that are growing in the water. Lift stones and swish under them, too.

Clear as much mud from your net as you can with one sweep of water.

Now gently tip the things left in your net into your dish.

No creatures at all means badly polluted water. This water is poisonous.

Lots of different creatures means clean water.

CLEAN WATER
many different creatures
in each scoop of water

lots of mayfly nymphs

lots of stonefly nymphs

DIRTY WATER
still many different
creatures but hardly
any nymphs

lots of chironomid
larvae

DIRTIER WATER
fewer than 5
kinds of creatures

lots of large
water snails

FILTHY WATER
almost nothing but
tubifex
worms

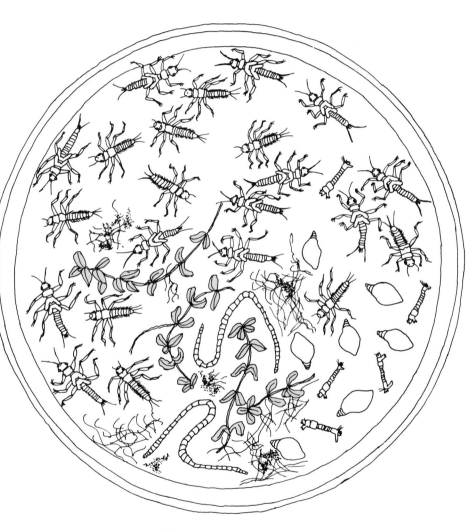

Test the water in three or four places along
the bank to check your results. Downstream
from a sewage pipe will be worse than
upstream.

MOVING AROUND

Getting from point to point in wild parts of the country needs careful planning.
It is always best to go in a group so you can help each other.

People can get lost just as easily on an afternoon's walk in fine weather as they can on a long trek in winter.

Even experienced bushmen never go into the bush without some safety gear and extra water and food.

You must be properly prepared. This means knowing where you are going and how long it should take you.

You should be able to cover 5 kilometres an hour on flat open ground. Allow about 2 kilometres an hour for travelling through rough or hilly country.

Look at a good map before you start. Most maps are drawn for cars. You want one that shows up the main landmarks and the kind of country you are walking through. Look for the main tracks and follow them.

Never set out without telling someone where you are going and when you will be back. This makes it easier for people to decide if you are safe or not.

When you are out in the wilds it is a good feeling to know that someone else knows where you are and where you are heading.

Remember that the weather can change very fast. It is nearly always colder than you think it will be. Plan carefully the clothes and shelter you will need for the worst kind of weather for that time of year.

Your food and water needs lots of thought too. An apple won't get you very far. Always take more than you think you will need.
A knife, some rope, a compass and a map are important even on short walks.

In very wild country it is a good idea to leave a trail behind you. This lets people follow your path easily.

A sharp stick can mark arrows on the ground as you go. If the bush is too thick, cut gashes into tree bark every now and then. Be careful not to cut too deep or you will hurt the tree.

You could snap small leafy branches sometimes too. A broken branch shows up clearly to someone with sharp eyes.

You want to know where you are all the time. This means that you could find your way back along the track you came – or easily press on to where you want to get to.

Moving around in wild places takes a great deal of planning and careful thought. You don't want people thinking you are lost and maybe sending out search parties for you.

Learn to be in charge of yourself.

When you are out in the wilds use your eyes. We often walk for long distances without noticing much.

Wild places can be very confusing. Trees and bushes and rocks and tracks can look the same after a while.

All the time you are walking think about the things around you. No two trees are really at all alike. The colour of the ground changes. The things that grow along the track change all the time.

Keep on the look out for special signs. You can learn to notice things that will help you find the way again.

Large patches of light-coloured lichen on tree trunks can be seen a long way off. Look for hollow logs, a burnt patch of forest, yellow fungi, a clump of wild flowers. These things mark your trail. Remember them as you go.

Practise this kind of bush walking whenever you can. You will find that your eyes get much sharper at spotting special signs. Your memory for things you have seen will get better and better.

MUD BRICKS

Try making your own bricks. If you have a good supply of mud, you can build a hut big enough for you or a large dog.

Test the soil before you start to make sure your bricks will last well.

Dig a narrow deep hole and mix up the soil from it. Soil forms in layers of different kinds and you need a mixture of them to test.

Fill one third of a straight-sided jar with some of the mixture. Add water until the jar is two-thirds full.

Shake the jar then wait until layers appear.

water

clay

sand and silt

coarse sand and stones

If you end up with just one layer of dark brown mud, try somewhere else for brick-making. You need at least half clay to make strong bricks that won't crack and crumble.

Make a wooden mould to shape the bricks. Building is easiest if all the bricks are the same size.

The bricks will be heavy to lift if you make them too big. A mould that measures 25 cm long, 20 cm wide and 12 cm deep on the inside is about right. Use 4 pieces of wood nailed together.

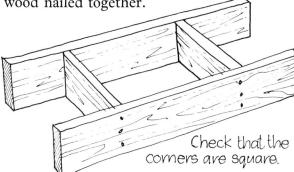

Check that the corners are square.

Dig a mud-trampling hole just big enough to move around in. Make it as deep as you can – but below your rubber boot tops.

Fill the hole with water and mix back the earth you have dug out. Start trampling to make the mud ready to use.

Add earth as you trample.

The mud should be wet-looking but firm enough to hold its shape in a tall pile. Chip in earth from the sides of the hole, if you need it.

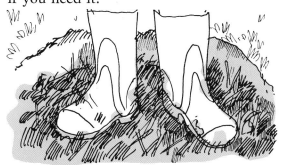

If your test showed lots of clay, add some pine needles or dry grass clippings to the mud. This will make stronger bricks. Dig them in well then trample some more.

Wet the mould and half fill it with mud. Press it down firmly all over. Make sure the mud fills the corners.

Shovel in more mud until the mould overflows. Press it down again. Scrape the mud off level with the mould.

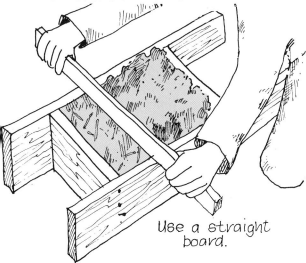

Use a straight board.

Now you can lift the mould off the brick. If the brick sticks, start again with more pine needles or grass clippings in the mixture. If the brick flops out of shape, the mud is too wet.

Clean the mould with a scrubbing brush before you make the next brick.

Lie the bricks on flat ground to dry. This takes about three weeks in fine weather. Turn the bricks after each week.

Cover wet bricks with plastic if it looks like rain.

When you are ready to build something, mix some more mud to join the bricks together. Use a thin layer between each row of bricks and on each brick end.

WATER DIVINING

Some people have a special feeling for water. They can tell where it is under the ground by receiving a kind of signal from the water through a rod into their arms. Farmers often use water diviners to show them the best place to sink wells or dams.

Maybe you are a water person. You will need to hold something in front of you that makes the signals from the water clear – rather as a TV aerial collects signals from a TV station.

Water diviners use all kinds of things for rods such as long pieces of wire, forked sticks, wire coat hangers – even a giant salami has been successful.

The forked stick is the most usual rod. Some people say that this should be cut from a large and shady tree just before it is to be used. But choose something you feel might be right for you.

Hold the rod out in front of you with both hands. Walk around slowly thinking of nothing but rushing water under the ground.

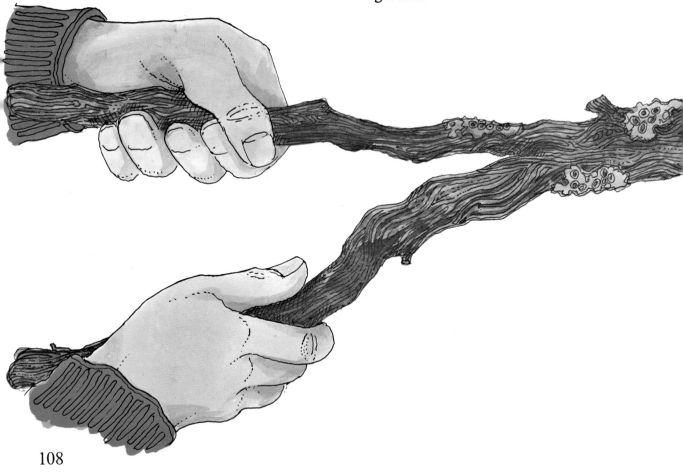

If your hands tingle or the rod jerks downwards there may be a stormwater drain, an unknown spring, or even an underground river beneath you. Try tracking its path.

POTATO

Plant a potato in a large bucket and with any luck you should get a bucketful in about 4 months. Early spring or fall is the best time.

Any large container will do but it must have drainage holes in the bottom.

Half fill your container with soil and mix in a little compost or complete fertilizer.

Make a hole in the soil large enough to take the potato, and cover it over.

leave the 2 strongest shoots on and rub the rest off

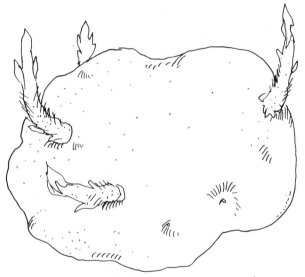

you might find a sprouting potato in the kitchen - or sprout one yourself

Choose a potato with lots of eyes. These are buds and some of them will begin to sprout if the potato is left in a light airy place for about a fortnight.

110

In 3 or 4 weeks green shoots will appear above the ground. Now add just enough soil to cover them again. This forces the stem to keep pushing upwards while little potatoes are forming along it below the ground.

Keep covering the plant until the bucket is full. The soil should be kept damp.

The plant will flower – a sign that things are happening underground. When the flowers die, stop watering. Potatoes will have formed and wetness might make them rot.

When the whole plant dies tip the bucket out and see how many potatoes you have produced.

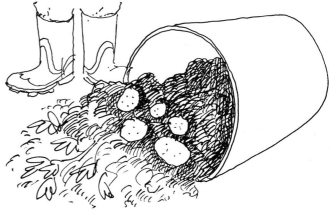

111

STREET CARNIVAL

A street carnival makes people cheerful. If they are enjoying themselves, they may throw you a coin or two.

For your carnival choose a time when the street is full of people. Near shops on a Saturday morning might be best.

Have lots of different things going on at once. Get some friends together to plan the carnival.

Busking is a very old way of raising money in the street. You can sing or play an instrument in groups or alone. People throw coins into a hat on the ground if they like the sounds you make.

Jugglers, acrobats and clowns can collect money in hats, too. Make crazy costumes to stand out from a crowd.

Have a joke and riddle booth. Make a booth to hold one or two people – choose your best joke-tellers.

Join large strong cardboard cartons together and decorate them with paint or coloured paper. People pay to hear a joke or riddle. It's too bad if they've heard it before.

People can pay to have their portraits drawn too. You will need a table and chair and lots of paper and coloured felt pens. Or use chalk on the pavement.

Do quick drawings of people's faces. Look for the thing that makes each one different – such as big ears, lots of hair or a long nose.

HOMING PIGEONS

Pigeons are home lovers. They can be taken hundreds of kilometres away and still find their way back.

People took boxes of pigeons with them to battle and on journeys long ago. When a traveller wanted to send news home, a message-carrying pigeon was set free.

Pigeons are not often used for carrying messages now radios and telephones have been invented. Faster and faster homing pigeons are bred for racing. A champion can fly more than 800 kilometres in a day.

You could train pigeons to carry messages for you. You will need a pair of young birds – one would get lonely. A pet shop is the best place to buy pigeons. Wild ones carry bugs.

Your pigeons will have been fitted with a message-carrying band a week after hatching.

The pigeons will need a dry, roomy coop. Build it where a flying pigeon can see it easily. The flat roof of a tall building is the best place but a clearing in a garden will do.

Get advice about caring for pigeons. They need grain, grit, greenery and fresh water every day. Clean their coop often and keep wild pigeons out.

A coop 1 metre square is big enough for 2 birds.

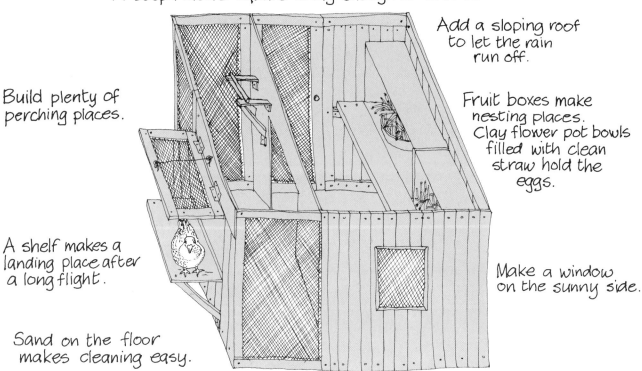

Build plenty of perching places.

A shelf makes a landing place after a long flight.

Sand on the floor makes cleaning easy.

Add a sloping roof to let the rain run off.

Fruit boxes make nesting places. Clay flower pot bowls filled with clean straw hold the eggs.

Make a window on the sunny side.

You and your pigeons must first get to know each other very well.

At feeding time give the birds some grain in your hand. Call the pigeons to their food by whistling. They will soon know the sound that means food and you.

Nesting time is best for training pigeons. They usually lay two eggs at a time, about seven times a year. The pair will take turns to sit on their eggs. If one is let out of the coop while the other is on the nest, it will always return to its mate.

Choose a fine still day for training. Let one pigeon out and scatter some grain in the coop. The pigeon will wander around for a while then return. When both pigeons are used to freedom try a short training flight.

Take one pigeon a short way from home – down to the end of your street would do. Carry it in a covered basket or box with a little grain inside. Let the pigeon go and it will fly home.

Gradually take the birds further and further away. After a while, you can take one for a long bus or train ride before releasing it. It might get home before you.

Pigeons get lost in storms and fog – so choose fine weather for flying trips.

After a year of training one of your pigeons could fly home from as far as 150 kilometres away.

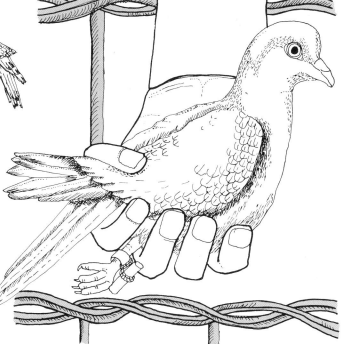

Write your messages on a small piece of paper. Roll it and tie it to the pigeon's leg band with a strand of wool.

Ask a friend to train a pigeon, too. You can exchange pigeons when you visit each other and send a message later.

BIRTH

Dogs and cats mate and give birth easily and often. But they can have happy lives without having litters.

If it is going to be hard to find homes for the young, your pet can be operated on to stop it breeding. Get advice from a vet about the best way for your animal.

If you are sure you can find owners for several kittens or pups, think about letting your animal raise just one litter.

If you see your female dog or cat mating, you can work out when the litter will be born. About 63 days from the mating is the length of time the young take to grow inside the mother.

Watch for the animal's belly to begin swelling. Her rows of teats grow bigger and pinker when she is pregnant too. This is the sign that the milk supply is getting ready.

Give your animal the best food you can now – lots of milk and high protein pet cubes as well as normal meals.

The animal knows when the birth is near. She will be restless and searching for a nesting place that feels right.

You could make a nesting box for your pet. But be prepared for her to choose somewhere else.

A large cardboard box makes a cat's nest. Line the box with a thick layer of newspaper. The cat will shred this with her claws. Make a round hole 15 cm from the bottom of one side. A lift-off lid lets you look inside.

A square box with sides about 25 cm high is best for a dog. Measure her when she is lying down and make the box 25 cm longer than she is.

Fill the box with straw or shredded paper. Trample it down in the middle.

Most animals like to be alone when giving birth. But a cat or dog who knows you well won't mind you watching quietly.

It can take hours for a whole litter to be born. Ring a vet for advice if you think the mother is trying hard to give birth but no young are coming.

116

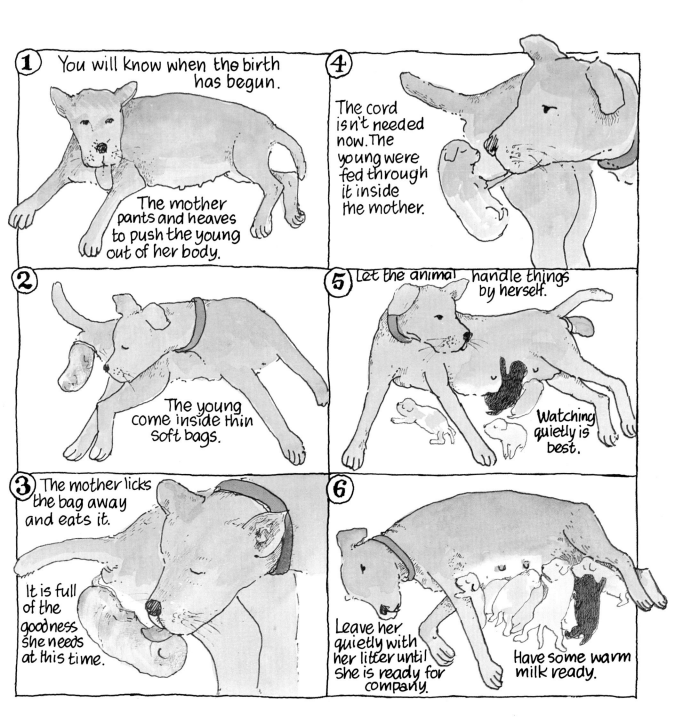

1 You will know when the birth has begun.

The mother pants and heaves to push the young out of her body.

2 The young come inside thin soft bags.

3 The mother licks the bag away and eats it.

It is full of the goodness she needs at this time.

4 The cord isn't needed now. The young were fed through it inside the mother.

5 Let the animal handle things by herself.

Watching quietly is best.

6 Leave her quietly with her litter until she is ready for company.

Have some warm milk ready.

117

AN OLD BIKE

Getting an old bike back on the road is a good thing to do.

Unless you are a real bike expert, there are some things that would make an old bike too far gone to fix. Check with a bike shop. If the frame is twisted or weakened by a lot of rust, or if the wheels are badly bent – look for another bike. If the bike needs a lot of new parts it may be cheaper to buy a second hand bike in good condition.

Check your old bike over carefully before you start and collect the things you will need – some grease, a can of light machine oil, kerosene, rust solvent, spanners to fit the nuts, maybe some new nuts, rags and newspapers.

Wash the frame with soapy water and a stiff brush to get off mud and old grease.

Take off the chain and soak it in kerosene for a few hours. Then scrub it clean with an old toothbrush.

If your bike hasn't been ridden for a while the wheel hubs may need cleaning and greasing. The wheels must come off for this. The back wheels of bikes with gears are hard to take apart – get advice before you start.

Before taking off the wheels turn the bike upside down on newspaper. Loosen the nuts at each side of the wheel. You may need rust solvent if they are stuck. Lay the wheel flat and take one side of the hub apart at a time.

Keep the pieces in a row on the paper so you will know how they go back. The ball-bearings in the hub let the wheel spin smoothly. Count them when you take them out as you must get them all back. Check them for cracks – you may need a new set.

Clean the hub parts with kerosene and wipe them dry. Pack the ball-bearing groove with grease.

Now all the parts can go back together again in the same order you took them off.

Check the tyres before you put the wheels back on. You may have a few punctures to fix. See if the ends of any spokes are poking through the inside of the rim – they make holes in the inner tube. Buy some new rim tape at a bike shop.

Hold the hub straight between the forks as you screw the nuts on tightly.

The headset and the pedals must swivel freely. Their ball-bearings may need packing with grease too. They are hard to take apart so get advice before you start.

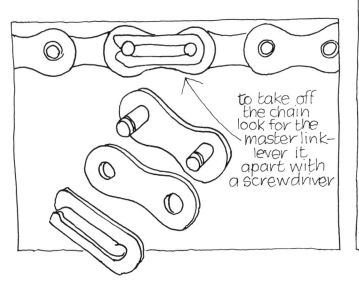

to take off the chain look for the master link-lever it apart with a screwdriver

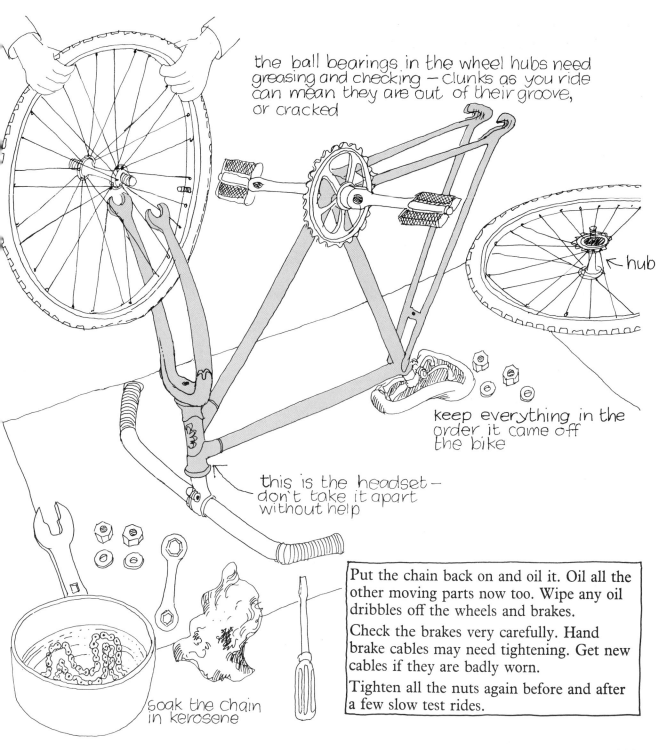

the ball bearings in the wheel hubs need greasing and checking — clunks as you ride can mean they are out of their groove, or cracked

←hub

keep everything in the order it came off the bike

this is the headset — don't take it apart without help

soak the chain in kerosene

Put the chain back on and oil it. Oil all the other moving parts now too. Wipe any oil dribbles off the wheels and brakes.

Check the brakes very carefully. Hand brake cables may need tightening. Get new cables if they are badly worn.

Tighten all the nuts again before and after a few slow test rides.

WILD PLACES

Keep your wild places safe. It should be hard to see where you've been.

Only light a fire for warmth or cooking and never in hot dry weather. Stay with your fireplace until the last spark is dead.

Take your rubbish away with you and pick up any you see left by other people.

Use dead wood for building shelters. Only cut green branches in an emergency.

Wild flowers soon die if they are picked. Save their lives by leaving them alone.

Careless people are the worst enemies of the wilderness that is left. In some areas they have to be kept out altogether so that the plants and animals can be saved.